WOOD

A RE-MEMBERING NOVELLA · HARDCORE SURGERY · DR FRANKENPEEN

CAT COLLINS

DRAMATIC FOOL BOOKS

WOOD

A RE-MEMBERING NOVELLA • HARDCORE SURGERY • DR. FRANKENPEEN •

CAT COLLINS

OTHER BOOKS BY CAT COLLINS

Diminishing Magic series
Paranormal Romance – completed series
JEWELS OF CLAY
FLAMES OF GOLD
GUARDIAN OF WHISPERS
RIPPLES OF GLASS

Reindeer Games series
Stand-alone Why Choose Christmas series about
Santa's Naughty Reindeer Shifters
FIXIN' VIXEN
Next book featuring a different reindeer – Christmas 2024

Curse of Between series
Stand-alone Urban Fantasy series featuring
two overlapping stories, one light and one dark.
READ BETWEEN THE GRINDS
Book 2 coming soon

Re-Membering Novella series
Each book a standalone
WOOD
Book 2 coming soon

Dedicated to everyone who ever wondered how many different words there are for penis in the English language.
I'm not entirely sure, but most of them are in this book.

And to the person on Facebook who asked for a "Magic Puppet" rec:
This is all because of you.

Content Information

Truth: Having Your Dick Severed Sucks

Chapter 1
Nico

The last thing I remembered before I passed out was the sight of my cock lying limp on the ice under O'Brien's legs. As far as last moments go, that one sucked a big dinosaur-sized dick.

If I *had* to be dismembered like that, at least it could've come at the hands of a beautiful, sexy, smart-talking woman instead of a bearded gap-toothed naked hockey player with a Stonehenge tattooed on his ass.

As my vision blurred, my last thought before I passed out was not for my dearly departed dick, but my brain had sailed straight to the most important question ever: Did we win the game?

I tried to ask as a dull buzz slowly brought me from my medicated slumber, but my mouth was as dry as the Sahara, despite the drool spilling from it.

Was I dead? Or just tucked away in some bunker made for the penally disabled?

"Thank Fuck, you're awake. How do you feel, Cap?" O'Brien scooted his chair closer to the bed. As he watched for signs of life in me, I realized it was much more comfortable than a hospital bed, but the tell-tale beep of machines and the IV in my arm told me that's where I was.

Great. Not dead, but the jury was still out on the penal dismemberment colony.

I opened my mouth. Nothing came out but a croak.

"That's okay. Don't talk. I'll fill you in." O'Brien muttered as he prepped his confession." First of all, I'm sorry man. I was so bloody drunk—we all were—and my skates got away from me when Anttila and Hodges collided. It was a tangled mess of limbs, so when the fastest skater in the NHL, that's you in case your memory's foggy, tripped and fell into me, I guess the force was too much and my blade sliced your schlong right off your body. The good news is you made the shot and we won the match."

Victory! Sweet!

He tugged on his red beard as he released a nervous giggle. "Guess we shoulda at least put on our jocks, huh?"

Memories began to flood into my brain in short bursts. Off-season, bachelor party, bourbon, tequila, hot waitress, more bourbon, sneaking into the stadium, daring the team to skate naked without the lights on.

Holy shit. Did I get my dick chopped off by a skate blade when we were drunk skating in the off-season?

Yup.

I jerked my hands, going down to check the goods, finding nothing but a wad of bandages where my manhood should have been.

There was no feeling *there*. None.

If I'd thought my mouth was dry before, that was nothing. Not only that, but a deep nausea churned in my gut. My dick was gone, and along with it my manhood, my identity, my future progeny.

"Woah, woah, hold up. You shouldn't be touching down there yet. Doc says you need a few more adjustment procedures and recovery time. Everything's still numb and healing now, but you'll be back to normal in six to eight months."

Back to normal? What exactly did that mean? I did my best to roll in the direction of O'Brien and managed to formulate one important word. "Dick?"

He scratched his head. "Yeah, about that. Remember we were drunk, okay? There was a heated discussion over which one of us would pick up your prick so it could be reattached. Not that I want a prize or anything, but I was the one who manned up for the job, so I guess that makes us *really* good friends now."

I growled, impatient for him to tell me how I got where I was and what the fuck was going on between my legs.

He tugged his beard again. "Anyway, when we got to the hospital, with your cock in a cooler full of Gatorade because it was the only thing we could find that was cold, the doc said there was a billion to one chance they could re-attach your cock and even if they did sew it back on, it would be more for aesthetics than function. You'd need one of those pee-bags and could forget about sex forever." He shuddered at the thought of it.

Me too. I was thirty-five years old, in perfect physical shape, at the height of my athletic career, and single.

No sex was a death sentence.

O'Brien continued. "We huddled up, trying to decide what to do and figuring out who was going to call your Mom and tell her that her baby boy had been dismembered when a crazy little German man appeared in the waiting room, giving us this card."

He handed it to me and I flipped it over finding a logo with a one-line sketch of a rooster that resembled a dick. Across the base of the rooster/dick was a row of obvious stitches. The words *Dr. Frankenpeen, Re-Membering,* and *Hard Core Surgery* encircled the drawing. The only other information was a phone number on the back. "What the fuck?" I screeched, my voice still weak.

"Yeah, I know it sounds ridiculous, but after he explained what he could do for you, we took a vote on it and decided it was worth the risk. The worst case was that it didn't work, but that's what you were already facing with the regular doc, so we consented to your treatment, hoping it would get you a working member."

It was so much to take in. I snapped my fingers toward the pitcher of water on the nightstand. He nodded and poured me a cup. As I slowly chugged, I let my brain process what he'd told me so far.

Which was insanity incarnate.

I needed a second to regroup.

We were in a nicely decorated room with rich, warm tan walls and the comforter covering me was a silky plaid thing that told me this was no ordinary hospital. Oh, and the stylized and framed paintings of dicks all over the walls were another indicator.

I closed my eyes to drink, not needing the visuals. When I finished my water, words came a little easier. "Where are we?"

"Not sure. His clinic is hush-hush, need to know. He only allowed me to come with you on his chopper if I was drugged. This is a very exclusive place shrouded in all kinds of security. Cloak and dagger stuff. He said it was due to the magic part of his procedures if you can believe that."

"I don't believe any of this," I grumbled.

"I didn't either until I saw it with my own eyes. Not *your* new dick, but he explained it all and showed me before and after pics of a dude who'd run into a similar problem as you—not with skates, but he'd accidentally speared his manhood with a pitchfork—and Dr. Frankenpeen had replaced his bloody cock with one made with...this is going to sound crazy but stay with me. It was made with antennae from colorful baby aliens."

I blinked, wondering if we were actually in a mental hospital with O'Brien the actual patient.

"I know what you're thinking—no such thing as magic or colorful alien babies and how the fuck do you work an antenna cock—I had the same thoughts, but he insisted I trust him and his procedures, so I asked for the contact info of that patient. I called to get the low-down and this guy could not stop raving about his new dick. He said it still worked in all the necessary bathroom and sex ways, only now he had a screw for a base and he could change out his antenna cocks to suit his needs. He has a straight rod, a curl, a circle, and a triangle. He said it was all kinds of kinky and enjoyable for him and his partners. He wouldn't stop raving about Dr. Frankenpeen changing his life, so I figured, okay, let's do this."

I managed to sit up, gripping O'Brien by the collar of his shirt, prepping to gut him for agreeing to this nonsense. "Are you saying I have an alien baby antennae for a cock now?"

A man walking into the room diverted me from punching my friend. He had albino pink skin and slicked-back white hair. His light eyes were looking through a pair of horn-rimmed glasses and his shirt and tie were a hideous combo of puke green and blood red. "No, no no, this is not correct. No two penises are the same. Your new member is made from the wood of a famous magic puppet. So much different than the alien antennae."

He tutted as shuffled over to my bed. I released O'Brien from my death grip. "My last name is Wood and you gave me a wooden dick from a magic puppet? You've got to be shitting me."

"Nein. No shitting here. I take great pains in selecting the very best and most compatible materials for my re-membering surgeries. It's the magic part of the procedure. Once I find a suitable replacement and use the special magic, the rest is medical science."

I heard him speaking, but I did not understand his words. I was supposed to be swallowing that magic existed, as well as alien babies with antennae, on top of the fact that I now had a magic wooden member.

I'm sure my mouth gaped open as he carried on like this was a normal conversation. "Your DNA was compatible with the puppet, so you now have the wooden penis sculpted from his nose, in particular. After a few more procedures where I reconnect the nerves and your balls so that you may enjoy ejaculation, you shall leave here with a fully functioning penis that will last long beyond the confines of time."

I leaned back against the pillow, unsure of how to think or feel. It was a lot. Too much. O'Brien gripped my shoulder. "I hate to run, but promised the guys to stay by your side until you woke up. Now that you're up to speed, I need to head back to San Antonio. The season starts next week. Coach will put you on medical until you're able to come back and play. Just take your time healing."

I sighed. With all the penis puppet talk, I hadn't even considered how close the season was. We'd been dumb to do what we did when we did. I was the consequence of that mistake.

At least the rest of the team was okay. I only did this to myself. "I guess I should say thanks," I muttered to him.

"Nah. Don't worry about that. Just heal up and get back to us as soon as you can."

After a quick bro-hug, O'Brien left me with Dr. Frankenpeen. Despite his wild-eyed look, the doctor patted my leg like a regular caregiver may have. He was no regular doctor, that much was clear. "I understand you must have questions and I will be happy to answer them for you, but now that you have awakened, I must ask for research to gauge the magic for your next procedures. This, okay?" I nodded. What choice did I have? "Are you sexually active in your everyday life?"

"Yeah, of course."

"And does this sex involve men or women or both?"

"What difference does that make?"

"Much. Do answer please."

"Women."

"I'll mark that down. Do you find yourself able to achieve erection when you wish?"

"Hell yes."

"And you do not have any problems with the ejaculate coming too quickly?"

"For fuck's sake. Do we have to talk about this shit? Everything was working as it should before the accident. I screwed the waitress in the back room before it happened and she had no complaints. That's that. Tell me what I need to know about my new dick, please. I have a hockey season to get back to." Fuck six to eight months, I wasn't going to wait around that long. Whatever the healing process was, I'd cut it. My team needed me.

"All in good time, Mr. Wood. Now if you don't mind, I want you to close your eyes and think of something that would make your penis erect."

Jeez. "Do I have to?"

"If you want this procedure to work, you must."

I sighed. "Fine." I did as he asked, letting my imagination run wild for a second and dipping into the ole' spank bank. It was certainly more appealing than thinking about my brand-new wooden tool.

Conjuring up a vision of that waitress and how I hadn't even tried hard to pick her up. She'd invited me, pulling me into the manager's office, shutting the door, and getting on her knees.

She was on a break, therefore in a hurry, going to town on my dick within seconds. The moans she made as she bobbed up and down were sexy and I was hard and ready within seconds.

I pulled her up, turned her around, and pushed her down against the desk, smacking her ass before I entered her wet depths.

Nearly forgetting I was lying in a hospital bed with a strange German doctor who re-attached dongs for a living, a strange sensation crept over me. Heat flushed through my body and I felt myself harden, which was weird as shit because I was numb down there.

It was different than normal. I'd even go so far as to say better. Harder and more tingly, which seemed like I would enjoy using it in this state.

I sensed a shadow cross in front of me, so I opened my eyes just in time to discover Dr. Frankenpeen holding one of those little hammers to measure reflexes. Before I processed what was about to happen, he whacked my new wooden dick with that hammer. I shouted, punching him in the jaw on reflex. "What the fuck, crazy bastard!"

When he got up from the floor, his glasses were askew. "I did this to show you that your new penis is essentially indestructible. The smack I gave you did not register as pain to you, did it? This is the first stage of the process. This new penis will be immune to feeling pain."

I didn't feel one ounce of regret for hitting the guy, though he'd been correct. I didn't feel it, I'd just reacted as though I had. "Great, so I'm permanently numb and won't be able to feel the sex you just told me to think about. Super. Thanks for your help, doc. Can I go home now?"

"No, no, no. You misunderstand me. Once I do the upcoming procedures, attaching nerves and improving conductivity, then layering in an extra sensitive sheath of your grafted skin, your wooden penis shall be more sensitive to touch than ever before, especially when aroused. However, it will also be impervious to further injury. Zink of it this way: the lighter the touch, the better the feel."

What he said sounded good, even if his means of explanation sucked. Once my breathing had returned to normal, he set his glasses back on his face. "Now, I shall knock you out and get down there and do more magic so that you can do magic in the bedroom later."

He laughed at himself while he flicked the dial on my IV. I was out in the next few seconds, even though the thought of creepy Dr. Frankenpeen down there in my business was disturbing.

Truth: Sex is Like Pudding

Chapter 2
Nico

Slipping into San Antonio in the middle of the night so no one would know I was back, I made my way home, finally. Six months in the wrong bed was messing with me. I was ready to get my life back.

I lived in a huge modern structure with lots of windows and cool angles. Before the accident. I would often walk around naked despite those windows but given the fact that I had a wooden dick now, I wasn't so sure.

It still looked like a regular—ahem, somewhat smallish—trouser snake, but damn it if the size didn't me feel all kinds of inferior.

My former dick had been…formidable.

Dr. Frankenpeen had assured me the size would not make a difference. He'd promised the act of ejaculation would be better for me and my partners. I doubted it, but when he told me he jerked me off while I was still under to gauge the flow and pressure of my orgasms to do me a favor, I wanted to believe it.

I shuddered to think about him playing around with me like that, but he'd said he wanted my first time feeling myself come to be exciting for me so he kept his technical and magic-induced sex sessions to times when I was out of it.

That was not a thing I wanted to dwell on. At all.

Ever.

Getting back on the ice would me feel better. The Tower needed their captain, number sixty-nine back in the game and I'd worked hard to get into playing shape as my member healed on the doc's private island. Both my body and my prick were in peak physical form.

Going off the injured list close to playoffs wasn't ideal, but the team had a winning season in my absence and I couldn't wait to get back to them.

That would be for the next day though. At that moment, I had another thing I couldn't wait for—solitude. After having spent six months with nurses and crazy Dr. Frankenpeen's nose in my crotch, it was going to be good to be alone.

I wasted zero time heading upstairs to my killer suite and grabbing a tin of Dr. Frankenpeen's special beeswax wood conditioner before I stripped. He'd told me to use it daily, and before I had sex, to avoid splinters. It was organic, edible, and considered a lubricant if another person was involved in the act.

While I didn't have a person—yet—I was anxious to come with my new wooden cock, so I hit the shower on and used my finger to get a big scoop of wax conditioner as the bathroom began to steam.

The scent was intoxicating. A mix of cinnamon and ginger and some other warm kind of spice. It was manly, but also delicate too. Arousing was the first word that popped into my head.

I took my new wood in my hand, marveling at the slight appearance of the wood grain. He'd explained that the skin covering the cock was grown from my own skin cells, but it was so thin I could still detect the woodgrain underneath it.

I had a very active imagination, so I didn't need visual aids or porn to get me going. I didn't like to keep that stuff around because if I did have a woman over, I wanted to be classy. With that in mind, I slathered on a bit of wax and closed my eyes, reaching into my memories for material. I came up with a night had with a very smart-ass puck bunny with great boobs and an even better ability to take my cock in her throat.

I rubbed the wax up and down my shaft, trembling at the sensation of my fingers. I'd gripped myself to pee hundreds of times since I had this new equipment, but it was a different sensation entirely to use a softer touch and let my hand glide with the wax.

Dr. Frankenpeen had been right. It was like every nerve ending I had was now turned up to eleven. Even though my wooden dick was continuously hard—and still immune to the feel of Dr. Frankenpeen's little demon hammer—I still felt the sensation of my cock getting harder from the inside, just like it had before, only…better. Magic mojo for damn sure.

It was wood and flesh and sensitive and hard and even though I would never forgive the guy for making it smaller than the member I was gifted at birth, I dug the sensation of my hand slipping over it.

My breath hitched in my chest as I took it a little farther, gripping and twisting over the knob as I pictured the puck bunny sprawled out in her bed with her legs giving me an open invitation to explore. She'd been so wet and ready, I didn't have to do much to work her up, just stick my fingers inside her pussy and pump. Her eager moaning echoed through my head.

Faster now, I jerked my cock, groaning and turning my back to slip into the hot shower. My skin nearly sizzled as the water hit me, but I kept on going, the wax having done its job. My wooden cock was smooth and my hand glided over the surface like it was velvet.

So fucking nice.

I slapped my hand against the glass, looking for purchase as I let my hand wander down to my balls.

It was a weird sensation to go from woody to pure flesh, but I found the juxtaposition to be intriguing from both angles and figured the next woman I got under me would too. I hoped anyway. I liked giving it as much as I liked getting it. Sex was better when both parties were into it.

Ramping up my pace because I wasn't going to drag this first time out, I let myself get carried away with the memories of her wetness, the way she told me exactly what she wanted me to do to her. "Harder. Yes, give me that hot rod just like that."

I was close to the finish line, moaning my agreement with this figment of imagination, "Fuck, yeah." Not two seconds later, my balls tensed, and the tingle that traveled all over me telling me I was ready shot through me like lightning.

I came hard.

Gale-force winds hard.

And it felt so damned good, I couldn't stop the verbal release that came with it. I said words I'd never strung together and probably made a few up too.

Opening my eyes, I tracked the gushing stream of cum as it sprayed from my new wooden cock and trickled down the shower wall.

The feeling was insane. Sensational. I was still riding it out a few minutes later, my skin tingling in the water and my pounding heart thumping against my chest with every thrust of my hips as I emptied everything I had.

Thank you Dr. Frankenpeen.

Even though it was a little on the small side, this wood was going to be epic.

The next morning, the press was all over the player's entrance to the stadium. Word had somehow gotten out. My educated guess was that our owner, Bubba Bettencourt had leaked the news. That man would do anything for press. Once he'd planned a big event to drop twenty-thousand dollars from our namesake, The San Antonio Tower.

People came out in droves for their chance to catch some money. Only, the dumbass thought the wind would blow the dollar bills away, so he used coins. He ended up sending twenty people to the ER, some due to the crowd going wild, some because they were pelted in the eyeballs by coins.

It was a nightmare, but he managed to find the one person in the crowd who gathered a good bit of coins and had him plastered all over TV, radio, billboards, and social media for weeks. The stunt was a failure, but you'd never know that by looking at the media.

It would be just like him to make sure everyone knew the Tower star forward was back in the game.

They'd have to wait though. I threw on my sunglasses and hiked up my Tower blue hoodie. Let them take their photos. I had some ice to carve before I spoke to them.

I entered the locker room expecting the guys to be gearing up but found an uneven banner with words scrawled in marker. At first, my heart was warmed that they'd gone to the trouble to welcome me back into the fold, but upon further inspection, I realized It read "Welcum Back, Nico, and Your New Pecker."

O'Brien and the guys at Parker's bachelor party had spread the word.

"You guys shouldn't have," I drawled, walking toward O'Brien with open arms but right before the hug, I swept his legs out from under him, and punched him in the stomach, knocking him flat on his ass.

He laughed. "I guess I kind of deserved that."

"No shit. You cut off my dick!"

"Yeah but think about it this way: you're now a medical miracle."

"He is not! He's a hockey player who's been on his ass for six months. Probably gained twenty pounds. If he doesn't skate well today, I'm benching his ass for sure."

Coach Anthony was scream-walking again. And dead wrong about the weight gain. "And another thing, he is not a medical miracle. I don't want any talk of his manhood outside of this locker room. You're lucky Bettencourt didn't fire every one of you for that stunt, but I'm guessing he didn't want to find a brand-new team. So, now we focus on us and the game. Everything else is inconsequential. Got it?" He didn't wait for us to agree before he said, "On the ice in fifteen or you don't play this week!"

I threw my stuff in my locker and started getting into my gear, trying to ignore the already-suited players lingering behind me or taking the long way around the room to get to the door.

Knowing I needed to get it over with, I turned around and dropped my drawers. "This is your one and only time to look. I hope it doesn't give you wet dreams tonight, fellas."

Most of the guys looked, uttered some kind of cock-related pun, and headed out. Thank fuck for that. It could've been a shitshow with the size of the thing. But, knowing my teammates like I did, I don't know why I'd been worried. They were great guys. Most of them anyway.

Fuck, it was good to be back.

Shrugging on the rest of my gear with a good attitude, and looking forward to my workout, I pushed out the locker room just as the whistle blew. "Alright, Wood, let's see if you've still got it."

I whacked my stick on the replica tower that stood at the entrance to the rink. It was a thing we all did before practice or a game. As soon as my blades touched the ice, I felt more at home than in my bed. The ice welcomed me back with no puns or snide remarks. Like I'd never left. I guess in my heart, I hadn't.

Practice went by like a blur and I was certain I was ready for the upcoming game. I felt pretty damn good as I headed to the locker room to change after an amazing practice.

I took the meds Dr. Frankenpeen had given me to increase nerve conductivity and started to change. Those pills, I assumed, were responsible for the extra sensations I got and I was going to take them like clockwork so that wouldn't go away.

I noticed a shadow looming over my shoulder just as I pulled down my pants. I turned to find Adam Fox staring down at me. He was a phenomenal goalie, which gave him a big head—no pun intended—and an inflated ego. "Your new dick's a little small, isn't it, Stick?"

I pulled up my pants and marched the few feet over to him. "Say it again, Fux, and see what happens."

"Look, I'm not trying to stir shit up. I'm just saying if you were getting a brand-new artificial member, why didn't you pick size XL? It's what I would do."

Of course, that's what I would've done too, but I didn't have the luxury of browsing a catalog for my new penis. It had been up to Dr. Frankenpeen and from what I could tell, he'd done me a solid. A smallish solid, but still.

Foxx was trying to mess with me just because he could.

I shoved him in the chest, knocking him back into a locker. I couldn't stand for the team asshole to ruin my good mood, "There's your answer then. I would never do what you would. You see, Fuxx" A poke to his forehead. He stumbled back, his eyes growing wary. "I don't need a big dick to speak for me. If all you have going for you is size, then you may as well quit."

As anger bubbled inside me, I was consumed with the need to put him in his place. Some might say I had a problem with anger management, but I preferred to think of it as an overdeveloped sense of justice for things I saw as wrong. Like, Foxx.

"Would you eat a cup of pudding with a shovel? Nope. You'd tear that shit up in a second. But if you used the right-sized spoon to curve around every millimeter of that cup, getting every delicious bit of that creamy gooey goodness from the edges into your watering mouth? That's far better for the cup and the mouth doing the eating."

Had I just compared sex to pudding? Yep.

I wasn't sure if I was hungry or horny. Probably both since I'd been thinking about that jack-off session since the night before.

Whatever the case, it did the trick to rid me of Foxx. He sniffed, threw me a face that said he'd won this little showdown, and headed out the door.

Asshole.

I'd been in such a great headspace after that practice and he'd just shit all over it. He just had a way about him that made my anger spike and brought out the worst in me.

Trying to cool down, I showered and got back into my civvies, hoping against all hope that there was a pretty and willing reporter outside ready to shove a microphone in my mouth and do me the courtesy of letting me shove something else in hers later.

Truth: Some Dicks Are Not of the Penal Variety

Chapter 3
Nico

None of the reporters qualified for my plans. While it sucked, I decided to turn the opportunity into something good and get some hype up for my return game, so I flashed my biggest smile and walked over to the horde of reporters, waving and giving high-fives to the fans and others gathered there.

The current hockey correspondent for ESPN in town to do pregame coverage was the first to grab my attention. "Tower Management has been tight-lipped about your whereabouts. Care to shed a little light on your recent absence?"

I had the urge to lay it all out for him and get it over with, but I tamped it down and tried to focus on what was important: the game. "All I can say is that I'm back and better than ever. Shine the lights on the ice Sunday and that'll tell you all you need to know."

"Come on, you've got to give us something, man? Were you ill? Was it a family matter? Mental break?"

I glanced over the crowd, spotting a sexy woman with long wavy black hair approaching the back of the group. She had her arms folded, pushing up her nice boobs in a pale yellow dress that made her olive skin glow.

Who are you, Beautiful?

Not a reporter, unless she was new. She looked too sophisticated to be a puck bunny, but she was definitely interested in what I was saying.

Movement beside her drew my attention. Fuxx had snuck into the crowd. My blood pressure rose as he whispered into the ear of one of the smarmy reporters who was his best friend.

Hunter Cato was an online streamer for some dumbass sports show called Sports Blender. He never said anything good or productive about sports ever and he had a dumb gimmick that he thought was hilarious.

How he managed to stay in business was beyond me. He and Foxx were friends, which made total sense in my mind. They were dickheads and I despised both of them.

As they whispered back and forth, they exchanged something, but I couldn't tell what had been in either of their hands.

Foxx had a bad gambling habit and it wouldn't have surprised me if Cato was his bookie or involved somehow. Those two were always up to some kind of questionable activities and couldn't be trusted. They deserved each other.

The raven-haired beauty beside them took a big step to her left to avoid them.

Good instincts, Beautiful.

I refocused, turning my attention to the ESPN mic. "Nothing big to report. I had an off-season injury that needed some rehab. I did the time, worked it out and now I'm one hundred percent ready for the ice."

"Speaking of rehab, I heard heroin was involved in the accident that sent you to rehab."

The bulk of the reporters turned to Hunter Cato, the man who'd launched the question. He was making his way to the front, eager to throw me off my game. Of course, Fuxx had prompted him. "It's fine to admit you have a problem, Wood. No shame in sharing your weaknesses."

I ground my teeth, hoping to get my boiling blood under control before I said something stupid. In the confines of the locker room was a safe space, but out here with fans and reporters was a different beast. "I agree that there's no shame in seeking help when you need it, but in this case, there's no need. I don't do drugs of any kind. I only drink in the off-season." Truth.

He pressed me, getting close enough for me to smell his stinky aftershave. No class, this guy. "I heard you and most of the team were high on the ice and your actions led to the death of a teen Tower fan."

This guy was insane. Where did he get this shit? Oh yeah, he made it up in his teeny tiny brain.

"There's no truth to that rumor whatsoever." There was also no truth in his statement about hearing that rumor. He and Foxx were setting me up. And the worst part about it was Foxx was only going to hurt his own team if he didn't step in and control Cato. Of course, he did no such thing, sneering on from the edge of the crowd.

A woman in the back, not the beauty, but another face I vaguely recognized as a newspaper journalist. "Then can you explain why you sent a huge condolence wreath to the funeral of..." she checked her phone, "...Andre Jones?"

Andre Jones. Andre Jones? He sounded familiar. I ran the name around my head, trying to put the pieces together. "Oh wait. Yeah, he was the Tower superfan who attended all the games. He passed away due to a car accident." Or maybe it was a motorcycle accident. I couldn't recall, but I knew it was months before the dick incident and the whole team had shown support like that. This woman was connecting dots where there were none.

"According to my sources in the Jones family, not only were you guilty of the accident that took Andre's life, but you also hit on his mother at the wake. Do you have an explanation for that?"

"What the fuck?" There was a collective gasp from the crowd as I uttered that choice phrase right in the ESPN mic. Not cool. "Excuse my language, but you'll have to understand that these rumors are unfounded. I'm shocked by these baseless accusations."

I leaned forward, making sure the ESPN and local news mics picked me up. "Listen, I'm here to play hockey and that's what I intend to do on Sunday. Everything else you're saying is nonsense. Let's turn the conversation back to the ice. The Blackhawks are playing well this season. It's going to be a great game."

I got a half-smirk from the beauty in the back. I guess she'd approved of the way I handled Foxx and the reporters he'd tipped off on some whacked agenda.

Hunter Cato took my momentary lapse of attention and stuck his phone in my face. "Just one more question. I promise it's about the game." I nodded, my body coiled tight on high alert. "Can you address the comments Bubba Bettencourt made at the NHL owner's roundtable press event last week?"

I clenched my hands, wanting desperately to punch this guy for that kind of curveball, but knowing I couldn't. At least not in front of all these people. Maybe I could corner him in a dark alley somewhere and share my innermost feelings with his jaw. "I can't comment on that because I haven't heard his statements, now if you'll excuse me I need—"

"He said the team was playing well in your absence and you'd always been a wild card off the ice—WildWood, he called you—so he was looking into trading you to the Flying Squirrels if you don't score Sunday."

My chest tightened in shock. I almost lost my fucking lunch all over the ESPN guy's shoes. If that had been true...

But it wasn't true. Sure, Bettencourt was a sanctimonious, pompous douchebag who thought his money and influence could dictate the actions of his team and employees, but he wouldn't get rid of his star player and captain just for failing to score in one game.

Cato went in for the kill with his next statement. "You scoring in any more games is an unlikely event considering the prescription drugs found in your locker this morning. The NHL will have your hide."

How was anyone believing the nonsense? Their accusations had changed from heroin to killing a teenager to hitting on a grieving mother, to prescription drugs in my locker. I opened my mouth. That's when Hunter Cato brought out the smoking gun.

"Check my website for photographic evidence," He called as he waved my bottle of nerve pills and a tin of my beeswax above my head for the crowd of reporters to see. "Fill out the form if you want to use my exclusive photos or I'll send you a C and D. The prescribing doctor's name is Dr. Horatio Frankenpeen. If that isn't a fictitious moniker, I don't know what is. He's using. This guy is his source. You can see it here."

Heat flushed through my body and I lost any ounce of good sense that I ever had in me. It flew right out like a bird. "Look you imbecile jerkwad, if you want to know what drugs I'm taking and why, I'll tell you. Since you're determined to undermine me out of a job, let's just get all the nasty cards out on the fucking table, shall we?"

It was for the best. Better than the world thinking I was a depraved drug addict who hit on grieving moms.

"Six months ago, my friends and I were skating drunk and there was a freak accident that led to my dick being severed by the blade of a skate. Yeah, you heard me. My cock was sliced off my body. I was taken to Dr. Frankenpeen, a specialist in the field—re-membering, he calls it—and I was given a prosthetic appendage. The meds he prescribed are to keep my new shaft in working condition so I can lead a relatively normal life. That includes mind-bending, feel-so-good-it-hurts sex with my fully functioning prick."

Even as I was spewing it, I knew it was the wrong choice—I'd used like six different words for penis in my tirade—but I was a freight train heading down the track to the truth and I wasn't going to leave any room for misinterpretation. Not with Foxx and Cato trying to derail me at every turn. They wanted to make shit up, well the truth was even more powerful and unbelievable than their lies.

"None of this has to do with Andre Jones, his mother, whom I don't know, or illegal drugs. The things you're holding are prescribed medications by a medical doctor. One's that you took from me illegally. I should sue your ass and Foxx for it."

The crowd was gaping in stunned silence at my outburst. One woman was escorting her child away and another was using her hands to cover her daughter's ears, while the reporters were typing or speaking into mics or blinking in rapid succession.

Not my brightest moment, but it felt good to get it out. Now that people knew, it would be fine and the other shit would fade into the background.

I hoped.

Then Cato broke into a creepy smile, looking like he knew he had me. "That's a great story, but it's pure fabrication. Bubba's going to fire you for this."

Which is exactly what he wanted all along. What Foxx wanted. To get rid of me.

What happened next I want to call a mental break from reality. I lunged at him, cold-cocking him with my fists, right then left. He fell to the ground blood gushing from his mouth and nose and I gave a satisfied smirk before I spat on the guy and trudged toward the player's entrance again.

The sound of camera shutters clicking was the soundtrack to my dramatic exit.

#NewJobNewRulesNewLaurel

Chapter 4
Laurel

I kind of felt sorry for the guy. He'd tried to handle the situation professionally, but he lost his cool and made it a hundred times worse. At least.

This was going to be a challenge.

He was sitting on a bench in the locker room, his arms folded, scowl on his face. He'd been through the wringer with the coach first, then had a call from Bubba Bettencourt that confirmed there was more on the line for him than he'd ever imagined.

He had to perform well, but beyond that, he had to toe the line in a way that men like him were not capable of. Bubba Bettencourt fancied himself a whale among sharks. He loved his money, but not as much as he loved his squeaky-clean, wholesome, family-man image.

Nico Wood had just shit all over that.

I *did* enjoy a challenge.

I buttoned my brand new San Antonio Tower blue blazer as I stepped into the locker room. It was a shame to cover up my stellar yellow dress, but if this was going to go well, I had to look and act like the professional I was.

I took a deep breath. If I didn't kill day one, my job would fly out the proverbial window along with Nico's.

Marching over with as much confidence as I could in the strappy heels I'd sadly chosen to wear, I stuck out my hand. "Hello, Mr. Wood, I'm Laurel Tyler, the new social media specialist for the Tower. It's nice to meet you."

His head slowly rose to meet my eyes and I was stunned speechless by the way the overhead lighting reflected in his pale eyes. I couldn't decide if they were blue or green, landing on aqua before he finally took my hand. "I saw you in the back of the crowd. I suppose you're here to scold me too." The corner of his mouth kicked up. Like the idea of that wasn't wholly unappealing to him.

"You were doing well until your temper got the best of you."

"Yeah, tell me something I don't know, Laurel."

He drawled my name out, like was trying to see if he liked saying it. It wasn't lost on me that the deep gravel of his voice and the way his tongue rolled over the L's was nearly orgasmic.

I wasn't going to go *there* though. No matter how attractive he was how soft his dark hair looked, how yummy he smelled, I had to stay within the confines of the professional realm. I was making a fortune on this job and I wanted to keep it, unlike the last one I lost because I'd stepped over the line, sexually with my client. I could not and would not do that again. Brand new me was a professional through and through.

Besides, lines and rules kept me safe. "You and I are going to be spending some time together in the upcoming days, Mr. Wood. Even though I was hired before your outburst today, Mr. Bettencourt has given me the task of overseeing your media profile personally while my assistants handle the daily work for the team."

His jaw was even more pronounced as he gritted his teeth. I bet he could do some beautiful damage with those things. "I'm sure you're aware he's a family-oriented individual and he wants me to help smooth over what happened today and transition you into the wholesome role model for the team instead of a man who screams about his penis and hits reporters."

"No offense, but I am who I am and I'm not going to change."

"None taken and I'm afraid you don't have a choice if you want to keep your job. You did some damage to the entire franchise today, but I can help you fix it. You just have to do what I tell you and keep your head down."

He stood up, taking his time to rake his eyes up and down my body with molten scrutiny. Yep, if I wasn't working with him, I would've totally allowed this guy to become my next mistake. His body was cut from granite and the way his smirk zinged right to my girly bits made me swoon. But since *that* wasn't on the table, I chose to ignore his heated aqua gaze and remain distanced from him.

Lines. Rules.

"I've done nothing but keep my head down for six months, Laurel. Every word I said today was the truth. I had a cock transplant. My new dick is wooden, by the way." He stopped to gauge my reaction. It took everything in my power not to shift my eyes downward, but I managed it.

A wooden cock. How does that even work? I mean, I had a plastic dildo, but wood between his muscular thighs? How? What about splinters?

Rules. Lines.

"What's underneath your clothes isn't my concern, Mr. Wood. I'm all about the image from the outside. Let's get to work. I've got some things already lined up to help with damage control."

He smirked. "Great. Can hardly wait for the exciting opportunity to polish my image into a vanilla, pompous puppet that smiles too much."

I bit my lip to avoid laughing. I couldn't begin to imagine Nico Wood fitting into that mold. Yet, it was my job to put him in it. "The sarcasm needs to go, Mr. Wood. It doesn't trend well."

Sighing, he put his hand on the small of my back to escort me to the door. Just the pressure of his fingertips seemed to fan all over my body. I opened the door myself, stepping away from him and trying to give him a serious look that said I meant business.

He grinned, which told me I needed to work on my serious face. "Fine. I promise not to be a sarcastic grump if you promise to call me Nico."

"I can do that, Nico."

"Fantastic. Now before we do whatever press junket you have lined up, I need to go get my meds back from Cato. I'm feeling like I might need the wax soon."

I wasn't sure what he meant by that, but if a doctor prescribed meds, they were usually necessary. His pace increased as I led him out the door to the employee parking lot. I'd never heard of wax medicine, but I'd never heard of a wooden cock before either.

I should've gone inside with Nico to get his meds back. Instead, I chose to multitask by letting him handle that while I sat in the car and composed a list of words he was not allowed to say publicly. I'd managed just over thirty words when he stormed out of the Sports Blender studio, which was just a converted closet in Hunter Cato's mother's flower shop.

Nico marched across the lot carrying a bag in one hand and a bouquet in the other. As soon as he slammed the door closed, I noted the knuckles on his right hand were bloody. "What did you do?" I screeched, dread flooding my veins. This guy was going to be difficult to handle if he couldn't stop slugging Hunter Cato.

"Exactly what I said I'd do: got my meds back."

I pointed to his hand. "Yes, but how much more damage did you make for me to clean up? We haven't even started yet. Hunter Cato has a big following for some reason and you hit him twice in one day. When this goes public—"

He interrupted me by putting a finger over my mouth. "He won't say a word. I just forked over a thousand dollars for a thirty-dollar bouquet. His mom is grateful and she'll make sure he tows the line. I saved you the trouble."

He handed the flowers to me. I hated to admit it, but there were gorgeous yellow tulips with unique fringy edges that would look perfect in my living room. "Here you go. I picked the yellow to match your dress. She said fringe tulips were a good choice for a woman who doesn't conform to convention."

I raised my eyebrow. He barely knew me, why did he assume I don't conform to convention? I couldn't stop myself from taking a big whiff of the flowers, but then I managed to take control of my composure. "I'm not going to thank you for buying me bribery flowers."

"At least thank me for doing your job for you. You're welcome."

Was he joking? "No, you weren't managing your image. You let your anger get the best of you again, then used your wealth to smooth it over. That's not going to fly, Nico. Not on my watch."

I put the car in gear and sped onto the road. Thankfully, no cars were coming. He was getting under my skin and we'd been together less than an hour.

I needed to get my shit together. "Here." I handed him my phone. "This is a list of no-nos. Words you can't say in public. Memorize it before we get to the next destination."

He took the phone and frowned. "Dick, cock, pecker, member, manhood, appendage, package, trouser snake, Mr. Happy, eggplant, rod, pocket rocket." Looking up at me, he shot me that devilish smirk. "Nobody says pocket rocket."

"Then you'll have no issue with that one."

"Mm. Let's see, what else do we have?" he drawled, his expression melting from anger to amusement. "Missile, joystick, peen, tube, schlong, dong, one-eyed snake, love worm, boner, willy, monolith…making assumptions with that one, no? Sausage, Dr. Feelgood, wiener, Johnson, anaconda, bulge, inchworm—"

I interjected, "You see, I accounted for both ends of the size spectrum."

"How politically correct of you. Continuing, we have shaft, jammer, rammer, knob, cum pistol, love saber, and finally dipstick." He laughed a good minute. "Who the fuck have you been dating?"

"None of your business." I snapped, hating how stupid my list sounded coming out of his mouth. I had my reasons for it though.

"Maybe not, but wherever you're finding your dates or boyfriends, go somewhere else. Outside of cock or dick, this list is nonsense." He handed my phone back, his lips shifting into a sexy smirk. "By the way, you forgot penis."

Cat Collins

Truth: Fighting Is the Best Foreplay

Chapter 5
Nico

As we pulled into the parking lot at Channel Five, I was mentally going over Laurel's entire list of words. I had no trouble thinking about it since my brand-new wooden cock was thinking about her.

She was a looker and even though she was trying to suppress her fire, I detected her smart mouth and fighting spirit already. I was going to have fun dragging her out of that steely professional shell she locked herself behind.

Yeah, my pocket rocket was preparing to launch.

After we passed through security and made our way to a small studio, she turned to me. "This reporter is a friend who promised to give you slow-ball questions."

"Are you sure you meant to say slow-*ball*? That feels like a no-no word." I mocked, raising an eyebrow and becoming enraptured at the pink flush of her cheeks. She kept from acknowledging my barb, but I could see how hard it was for her.

How hard *I* was for her.

It had been a while since a woman had captured me so fully and so quickly, but this was no regular woman. I wanted to know more about her as much as I wanted to know her in a carnal way.

"You know what I mean," she huffed, folding her arms across her chest. "This interview will hit the air tomorrow morning, so speak about the incident in the past tense and use the word 'yesterday.' Your official answer anytime the outburst is mentioned is that you accidentally took cold medication and it had an adverse reaction with the meds your doctor prescribed for the hamstring injury you've been recovering from. You went home, got some rest, and stopped the cold medication. You apologize for the situation and say you've discontinued the cold stuff. Everything is copasetic for the game Sunday."

Wow. She'd certainly thought it through.

Too bad.

"I have problems with this. One, hamstring injuries last seven to eight weeks, at most, not six months. Two, I don't have a cold and nobody buys that feeble excuse anyway. Three, I'm nothing if not honest. I'm actually glad the info is out there now. We can start focusing on the game at the same time as normalizing talking about this stuff in the media. It could help people who suffer from groin injuries."

She seemed unaffected by my words. "Add groin to the list."

"Come on, Laurel." Fuck, I loved her name. I couldn't wait to say it with my head between her legs. "It is what it is. I'm not embarrassed and I don't see a reason to hide it. Sure, I could've been more delicate in my delivery before, but I don't want to lie about this anymore."

She shook her head. The way it made her hair swing gave me all kinds of ideas. Mainly, the thought that it was long enough to grip in my hands. "You must be the last man in the world who'd choose honesty. I can admire that, but from a job standpoint, if you don't do what I say, you'll wish you were playing for the Flying Squirrels. Bubba Bettencourt is dead serious. You need to be too. From this moment on, you're my puppet and I'm pulling your strings."

While she did have a point about Bettencourt, I wasn't sure it was as dire as she made it out to be. I wanted to argue my point more, but her reporter friend joined us and the mood shifted. They spoke for a minute, as I watched her work to help me, then I was escorted to the set.

The reporter guy, Scott Something, was like every other reporter in the world. Fake smile, white teeth, overhyped, and vacant-eyed. He started the interview by asking about the upcoming game with the Blackhawks and how I'd prepared for it. I could answer those kinds of questions in my sleep.

When he segued to the injury, I glanced over at Laurel. She bit her lip, waiting for my response. Oh, that was a good look on her. My cock wiggled in response. "Well, Scott. It's a little *hard* to talk about. At the time, I'd been busy with the team and endorsements, working out, you know, a lot of *balls* in the air, so I was walking around like a *limp noodle*. Really, I was so overworked and tired that I was about to *go down*.

"So, to get some of that off my mind, I went on the ice to *take care of myself*, and get my *juices* flowing again, and I didn't warm up as I should've. As a result…" I paused, glancing up at Laurel. She was about to lose her shit trying to figure out if I was going to do what she said or not.

Man did I want to tell the truth. Just to see her explode.

But she wasn't wrong about Bubba and my career. I wasn't willing to play around with that.

"...I ended up severely injuring my hamstring and breaking my ankle in the process. I know, hard to believe for a pro skater, but accidents happen. I was lucky that I was allowed to heal in a remote location on Tower owner, Bubba Bettencourt's dime. I'm all good now, eager to show everything I have out there on the ice on Sunday."

The rest of the interview was a blur. I was mostly keyed in on Laurel and what she'd say or do about my answers. When Scott finally finished and we got into the hallway where no one else was around, Laurel marched in front of me, putting her hands on her curvy hips. "You didn't do what I said."

"Beg to differ. I didn't use any words from your list."

"Yeah, but the sexual innuendos were obvious. I'm surprised you didn't drop a well-timed *good girl*."

"Glad you picked up on that." I put my hands on her hips, picking her up and moving her out of my way. "Now be a good girl and tell me what's next on the agenda."

I kept walking, so she had to run to keep up with me, nearly slipping when one of the straps popped on her shoe. To her credit, she didn't even acknowledge it, she just kept marching and clicking those heels. "What's next is that you save the dirty talk for one of your puck bunnies and stop shrugging off my suggestions. There are lines we don't need to cross when it comes to social media and you're going so far over them, you need a telescope to see them. It's...fucking annoying."

I had to suppress a laugh. She was heated and so damn cute. "I'm not trying to annoy you, but I can promise you I will start if it makes you this flustered. You've been warned."

She was silent the rest of the way to the car. Oh, she wanted to give me a piece of her mind, that was for damn sure, but she reigned it in.

It ate me up that she was filtering her words. I wanted to play with that fire I knew was lurking under the surface.

I reached her car way before her. Made sense due to her broken shoe strap and my long legs. She hobbled lop-sided as she stormed my way, with a steely expression on her pretty face.

33

Taking pity on her, I jogged back and hoisted her over my shoulder. "What are you doing?" she squealed.

"Helping you." I carried her over to the car and opened the passenger side before setting her down. "Let me see your shoe."

I slid into the seat and turned. She reluctantly placed her foot on my knee so I could examine the broken strap.

"I have super glue in the glove compartment if you want to make yourself useful for once."

I definitely wanted to be useful to her—in so many ways—so I got the glue out, then took her leg in my hands, twisting it slightly so I could see the offending strap. "I'm very useful in certain capacities. Just saying."

My eyes were drawn to a small tattoo on her ankle. It was a tiny fairy with a blue dress and wings with the word "Bleu" in scrolling letters above it. "What's this about?" I ran my thumb over it, wrapping the rest of my hand around her ankle. "Did you forget how to spell blue?"

"Hilarious. Did you forget how to act like a civil sports pro—" Her breath hitched as I skated my hand over her shin and back down. Her skin was soft and inviting and the shape of her calf alone was making me ache for her.

She'd totally lost the rest of her word as I fanned my fingers over her skin. Swallowing, she stuttered to answer my question, watching my hand as I skimmed. "Sh-she was my cat. I got her in Middle School when I was obsessed with Paris and all things French."

"Hm, and the fairy?"

She rubbed the back of her neck. "That part's a little embarrassing."

"That makes me want to hear it even more." I lifted the broken strap, finding where it needed to be connected, but keeping an eye on the tattoo. "Be still." I applied a dab of glue, looking up at her and nodding for her to continue. "You've heard me spout a dozen different embarrassing things all day. The least you can do is return the favor."

She sighed, tracking my fingers as they played over the arch of her foot in my process of lining up the strap. "Fine. Don't laugh. Before Bleu died, she went a little cuckoo. She'd wake up from one of her cat naps and swat at the air around her, though there was nothing there.

"It was disconcerting to see the cat I had loved so much lose her mind, so I made up a story to help me feel better about her condition and impending death. I just told myself she was playing with fairies that I couldn't see. It made it easier to accept her passing when it came."

I pressed on the strap, fastening it to her shoe. "That's not embarrassing. You were a kid. It's cute."

"I was in college."

"Oh, okay, that *is* a little embarrassing." I bent down, blowing on the glue to dry it, noting the way goosebumps erupted on her legs as my breath tickled her skin. "It's still cute."

When her tongue slicked over her bottom lip, I had half the mind to pull her inside the car by the leg and let her experience my new member or whichever no-no word she wanted to call it.

But I checked myself.

There would be time for that, hopefully. She didn't seem like the kind of woman to do wanton fucks in cars. Nor did she seem like the type I usually hooked up with— eager puck bunnies or women looking for free meals. No, this woman deserved finesse so I wanted to take my time before I went straight to devouring her pudding.

I really needed to eat something.

With the glue dry, I took the opportunity to trail my hand up her leg again, feeling that luscious softness. I stopped just as my hand disappeared under her dress, tickling the back of her knee with my fingers.

That was a very sensitive place and her reaction to my touch was obvious. Her goosebumps got goosebumps and that little intake of breath was everything. "So, what's next on the agenda?"

There was a beat of silence that seemed to echo across the parking lot, but it was gone before I could capitalize on it. She cleared her throat and removed her foot from my knee, striding over to the driver's side with her heels clicking across the pavement. "Thank you for fixing my shoe." With her hand on the car door, she pointed at me. "What's next is that I am with you every second of every day until Sunday. You don't go anywhere without me. You don't talk to fans, pick up slutty puck bunnies, go to practice, or even so much as shop for groceries without me. I'm your shadow. Got it?"

"Yes ma'am. I'm your puppet. You're my shadow. Will you be lacing my skates too, or do you think I can handle that myself?"

35

The next morning she picked me up early. This time she'd opted for snug black pants, a purple sweater, and flat shoes, no straps in sight. She stood in my foyer, eyeing the black and white photo of the Tower I'd taken and had enlarged to put over my mantle. I could tell by the look on her face she was into it and the glass sculptures I had placed around the room, but she stayed mum. Of course, I poked at her. "What do you think? Designed this all myself. I took the photo of the Tower myself."

Her eyes widened. "You didn't hire a decorator?"

"No. Why would I want someone I don't know to arrange my space? It wouldn't be mine then, would it?"

She stood in the middle of the room, studying everything with a different eye, like she was trying to get to know me based on the color of the rugs and how much artwork I had. I left her to ponder and set the alarm code then headed for her car and threw my duffle in the back seat before climbing into the front. She ran to catch up and started in on me before she even got fully in the car. "Is that what you're wearing today?"

"You don't approve of my Tower hoodie and gray sweatpants?" I shifted in my seat, sticking out my hips to highlight my wooden friend. I might have been going crazy, but it felt a little bigger than it had the day before. That could've been thinking about Laurel.

"It's not that I don't approve, but we have public events today." For the first time, she looked down at my crotch, flicking her eyes back up quickly. "You need to look like a professional hockey player, not a weekend frat boy going to buy beer."

I laughed. She definitely approved of the bulge in my sweats if that rosy glow on her cheeks was any indicator. "This is what hockey players look like, but if it makes you feel better, I have nice clothes at the stadium. I'll clean up for you as soon as practice is over." She nodded, put the car in gear and we were off without another word about it.

I couldn't help but notice her stealing peeks at my crotch on the way. "You might want to keep your eyes on the road," I offered.

"What? They are." She gripped the wheel like I figured she wanted to grip my cock. Or maybe that was just wishful thinking.

Knowing I'd piqued her interest, at least a little. The rest of the way we sat in silence. When we stopped in the lot, I shifted toward her, hooking my thumb in my waistband. "Do you want to see it?"

She backed away against the window, as far as she could get from me. "What? No. I can't…I mean…I don't want to see your wooden peen! I'm your social media manager, not some puck bunny." She fumbled with the handle for a second before getting free, jumping out of the car, and heading for the door. This time I trailed along behind her, laughing to myself that I'd caused such a reaction.

She swung the door open. I caught it in one hand and stepped into the doorframe, blocking her ability to go inside. She looked up at me with wide dark eyes. That flame was there inside them. I could see it fighting to get through. Leaning down, keeping my voice as a gravelly whisper in her ear, "I know you're curious and I'm offering to show you so you'll understand what I'm working with. It might help you in scripting my lines. Or maybe understanding me a little."

She reached up, gripping the pocket of my hoodie with a clenched hand. For a nano-second, I thought she was going to pull me down and kiss me, but I wasn't that lucky.

Realizing what she was doing, she gasped, stepping back and smoothing out the wrinkles she'd made with her fists. "That would be highly inappropriate and unnecessary. You should go or you'll be late for practice."

Maybe it had been wrong to get her all flustered like that, but it sure had been fun. I thought about it all during practice. I didn't even let Foxx get to me because I was so wrapped up in thoughts of her and the way her blush crept on her cheeks and that glow she got when she argued with me.

However, when Foxx shoulder-checked me in the locker room afterward, I nearly broke his finger.

Goalies didn't need those all that much.

After I showered and dressed in a black sweater and jeans, I headed to the back private lot where I was meeting Laurel. She'd insisted on a moratorium on press for a while, so we were avoiding the gaggle of them who'd gathered at the normal exit.

Again, she was after me before we got in the car. "Did you hurt Foxx?"

"No. I just gave him a nice friendly hand-shake, that's all."

She growled in frustration. That sound would be the next deposit in the spank bank. "Stay away from him and keep yourself in check, Nico. You're making this har—difficult."

She got in the car and I joined her, leaning across her to pull her seatbelt and lock it for her. Since I was close to her ear, I purred before I spoke. "He started it."

Pushing me away first, which got me all kinds of hot, she shouted. "You sound like you're five. Just focus on being what I want, I mean what Mr. Bettencourt wants the rest of the day, okay?"

"Do I get ice cream if I promise to behave?"

Ignoring me, she practically peeled out of the lot and down the road, taking her frustrations out on the car and how she drove it.

As we made our way to wherever I began to see her silence for what it was: she was tossing ideas through that brain, trying to find the angle or the response that would best suit her needs. Or my needs, I guessed. She was thinking everything through to the most minute detail. I imagined it was exhausting.

"Have you ever done anything spontaneously?"

"Of course, I have." She turned down a street I hadn't even seen before. I had no clue where we were going.

I put my arm over her headrest, angling toward her. "Okay, what was the last spontaneous thing you did without thinking it through?"

She was quick with her answer. "I took this job."

I laughed. "Are you saying you wish you hadn't?"

Again, a pause. Thinking, thinking, thinking. "I wasn't until I met you, but that doesn't matter now. We're here."

Ouch. Burn. Why did that turn me on?

She got out her phone, typing furiously. "I need access to your social media platforms. For the foreseeable future, I do all your posts."

I didn't social media much. I had logins but only Twitter posted or uploaded when the mood struck me. Giving her access wasn't a big deal, though she didn't know that. "How do I know I can trust you with my passwords?"

"I'm your social media advisor. It's what I do."

"Yeah, but what if you post something off-brand for me and I don't like it."

She bit her lip, a sure sign I was getting somewhere. "The only brand you have right now is what Mr. Bettencourt tells you to have. Give me your info so I can do what he wants for you and we can get on with this. If you are so worried about trusting me, change your passwords temporarily and change them back when we're done."

There it was. A tiny bit of her flame rising to meet me. "No need to get so testy. I was just asking. My username and passwords are the same everywhere: NicoWood69, password CupofStanley, exclamation point."

She sighed. "You can't have sixty-nine in your username."

"Why not? It's my number."

"It's sexual in nature."

"Sure is. And?"

"For the last damn time, we are trying to make you into a wholesome, family-friendly guy."

"Yeah, good luck with that. For the record, my birthday is June ninth. You can spin it to that if it makes you feel better."

Jumping out of the car, I looked around. We were in the parking lot of Ed's Family Grocery. There was a crowd of kids and moms forming around the entrance, most of them in Tower gear. Laurel slammed her door. "Get those pearly whites ready to smile, Nico. Time to endorse toothpaste and hand out Whalies cereal, for a healthy fortified breakfast!"

The Whalies I got. It was Bettencourt's empire. We gave out so much cereal over the years. Kids lined up for that stuff, which I never got because it tasted like sugar-encrusted cardboard.

She shot off like a cannon and I hurried to catch up with her. "I'm a hockey player, not a dentist."

"Yes, well you're one of the few hockey players on this team with all your teeth intact. You have a nice smile and you need the public to focus on something other than what's in your pants, so we're going to point them way above your belt."

For the love of all that is holy, this woman was maddening. But she wasn't wrong. I'd been told my smile was disarming. I flashed one at her, one aimed to kill. "Lead the way, Shadow."

#LifeIsACircus

Chapter 6
Laurel

Nico was charming. He knew just how much flirt to put in his actions to make the women feel special and buy the product. But at the same time, he was respectful and didn't cross any lines physically.

So, he *could* behave.

I was sure endorsing toothpaste and pimping cereal wasn't the way he wanted to spend the day, but by giving the kids pointers and passing out free Tower pucks too, he seemed right in his element.

He didn't need me. Not really. He just needed a keeper for his temper and someone to smooth his naughty edges.

And the thing was I didn't blame him for his angry outbursts. He'd been through a lot. His freaking cock had been severed and he was walking around with a magic wooden replacement. I'd be angry too. However, there was more to him than anger. He was charismatic, funny, great at his sport, and he knew himself very well. That was the most enviable thing about him.

Other than his looks.

I should've taken him up on his offer to peep in his pants.

No. I should not have. He is your client.

Keeping it professional. Always.

Lines, rules. And walls too, for added protection. I couldn't let him get inside mine, no matter how high he turned up his charm.

After the crowd died down, he sauntered over, snagging a few boxes of toothpaste and throwing them in his bag. "Where to next, Shadow?"

"Do you have to call me that?"

"Let me think… yes, I do."

I wanted to hate it, but deep down I didn't. And that worried me.

Our next stop brought us to Laser Circus. My assistants, Jo and Joe, had called to say everything was all set and ready. One of Mr. Bettencourt's rich pals was coaching a group of kids and they'd spent the past month meeting and learning about teamwork and his "camp" was culminating in a celebratory game of laser tag. Nico was on tap to coach one team and Bettencourt's friend would coach the other as they battled it out and worked together to show what they'd learned about teamwork.

It was a chance for Nico to not only have a great photo op and social media blitz but also to score a few points with Bettencourt.

"Remember these are eleven-year-olds, keep it kid-friendly."

"I can contain my potty mouth if I want," he quipped.

I cocked my head to the side. "Can you? Let me just remember the first thing I ever heard out of your mouth..."

He grinned. "I have the urge to smack your ass for that, but as you requested, I'm showing restraint." He bounded out of the car, as eager as I imagined some of the boys being. "This is the best thing you've set up for me so far."

I had trouble keeping up with him because of those damned long legs, but by the time I did, he was already inside the building shaking the coach's hand and high-fiving the kids.

The entryway was set up like a circus tent with neon red and white stripes with clowns and lions and acrobats, all with garish circus music playing in the background. The team was already wearing the laser harnesses, which I thought would be a great photo opp. "Put your harness on and pose with the team."

Nico took a harness from a hook behind him and walked toward me as he fastened the gear around his muscular chest. "And here I thought you might want me to take something *off*."

"Please," I hissed. "That's exactly the kind of thing you can't say around kids. Or me, for that matter. We don't have that kind of relationship. I'm a professional."

He shrugged like it didn't matter much to him, then smiled wide as I took the photo and made the post.

NicoWood69: Teamwork makes the dream work! Playing a round of laser tag today with some future All-Stars! #SATower

Nico peeked over my shoulder as I hit submit. "Aw, I'm so nice. And vanilla."

"What would you have said instead?"

"Um, let me see, I'm about to blast some rugrats into oblivion! #NoMercy #DoYouKnowWhereYourChildrenAre"

"And this is exactly why you're not allowed to post. Now get in there and play. Let the kids do most of the work."

"Where would the fun be in that, Shadow?" He called as he ran over to the coach who'd moved over to a bench, rubbing his knee and wincing.

"My gout is acting up, so this is going to be rough on me. Take me out first so I can sit down.

Nico slapped his back. "No worries, Man. You can put in your sub."

Before I knew what was happening—because I was the fool who was looking around the entryway for another person who appeared to be with the team—Nico had swiped another harness and was strapping it on me.

"No. I can't play laser tag!" I protested.

"Can't or won't?"

The last strap clicked into place. "Both."

"Yeah, I'm not buying that, are you boys?" All twenty-two of them had crowded us to see what was going on, eager to get inside. Nico turned to whisper to the group and before I could protest again, the whole lot of them were giving me puppy dog eyes and sad faces. A few of them even dropped to their knees to beg.

There was no way I could refuse that and he knew it.

Damn him and that stupid smirk that seemed to have taken up a permanent residence when I was around. "Fine. I'll play, but you shouldn't expect too much from me."

There was a resounding cheer and I found myself captain of the white team facing off against Nico and the kids wearing red harnesses.

We entered the proper laser arena to get in place for the game. It was set up with three huge colored rings in the middle with obstacles like clowns and lion cages and things to hide behind and around. There was even a seating area around the perimeter that held spots for players to hide in and a catwalk and tunnel system designed to look like trapezes and a tightrope positioned above us. The whole thing was overwhelming and chaotic and I was sure I was going to leave with a glaring headache if nothing else.

Although I was determined to beat Nico.

I gathered my team around me. "Okay, I'm not a coach so what do you guys think our strategy should be?"

To their credit, they took turns and waited to hear all the ideas from the whole team before choosing the dark-skinned boy who said, "Blast the poop out of Nico first, then kill the rest!"

Sounded good enough to me. Except that it wasn't going to play well media-wise if they took him out of the game early. "Can I propose a counter plan? What if we shoot at everyone but Nico, taking out the smaller ones and leaving the big target for the easy win?" The boys nodded and I was pleased about my own plan to snap a few action shots during our game.

I adjusted my harness just as the fake ringmaster announced the game had started and the giant clock started counting down.

Nico came bursting forward, imitating a lion by roaring and snapping his teeth. At the same time, some of his team scurried to the top levels where the catwalk trapeze was hanging.

Feeling like an army general using hand signals to the boys on my team, I pointed toward the moving targets and they began to fire.

When Nico realized none of us were going for him, he shook his head. "I see you, Shadow. I know what you're doing."

I peeked around the creepy clown car I was hiding behind. "I'm playing the game just like you asked, Puppet." He shot a few blasts in my direction, but my reflexes were quick and I managed to dodge them. Frustrated, he released what was supposed to be a lion's roar I think, but it sounded more like a sexy growl than anything and I had to take a deep breath to keep from imagining how that sound might be used in other places.

Managing to lock Nico firmly behind my wall of professionalism, I shot a series of blasts aiming at kids in one direction, then rolled the other.

I had not rolled on the floor since...had I ever rolled on the floor? I couldn't remember.

I also couldn't remember when I'd had so much fun.

The kids were awesome, protecting their leader and taking lasers for me as we played. They had a blast and didn't get discouraged if their lights were triggered. They simply walked off and cheered their team on as the game progressed.

When the last kid on my team was tagged by Nico, I took the opportunity during the cheering and chaos to sneak into a tunnel disguised as a cannon on the far edge of the rings.

Nico was posturing and making a big deal to encourage the kid who'd been hit, but when he realized it was down to the two of us, he spun around. "I'm coming for you, Shadow. You can't hide from me."

I pressed my lips together, not wanting to give myself away, then scooted forward, peeking out of the cannon to see if I could track his movements. When I hadn't seen him for almost two minutes, I decided he was likely making his way toward me by going through the fake stands, searching the hidden spaces one by one.

I laid on my back and got my head and most of my body out of the cannon quickly, preparing to surprise him by sliding out halfway and firing, but before I could make that move, he surprised me. "Gotcha! You're dead, Laurel. You may as well give up."

Nico's rich rumble came from above me, making it obvious he'd climbed on top of the cannon—even though a sign expressly said it was forbidden— and was straddling it like it was a horse. Damned long legs.

Damned rule breaker.

He truly would have me if I moved more than a couple of inches and exposed the laser pad on my chest to him. There was no way for me to go back down to the other end of the cannon either because he had the advantage of being above me and could easily see me crawl out.

He had me.

I did not want him to win.

I did not want to miss the picture of him straddling that cannon either, so I pulled out my phone and raised my hand, hoping I was hitting the right button. There was no way I could use that photo on socials, but even from the minimal viewpoint I had, he looked so sexy with his hair disheveled and long legs stretching over the cannon making his thighs tight in his jeans, I couldn't let the opportunity pass me by. He shouted when I snapped the photo. "Hey, blinding me is not part of this game."

"Says who?"

"Says me. Now come on out and let me blast you with my love gun. You know I have you."

"Or I have you," I teased. "All I have to do is slide out and fire first."

"True, but I wonder which of us has the quickest reflexes: professional athlete or someone whose job requires her to be on her phone all day."

Okay, yeah, he probably had me there. I would be the clear winner when it came to fine motor skills like texting or typing, but he likely had the advantage when it came to his laser gun. And he was sitting in a better position to shoot.

Unless…

I slowly slipped back inside the cannon fully. The scrape of his gun and body as he scooted back toward the other end of the cannon told me he assumed I was going to try to sneak out the way I'd come in. He'd be wrong about that.

I rolled over, placing my belly, therefore my laser pad, underneath me. What I was attempting was a touch dangerous, but I was committed to beating him. I couldn't wait to see the look on his face when I did.

When the shuffling was nearly at the far end of the cannon, I used my legs to catapult me out. I pushed off with my toes and rolled forward, somersaulting as I hit the ground. Then I swung around and aimed. Nico was staring at me with his mouth gaping open, calculating a second too late. I fired and his red laser lit up just as he rocketed off the cannon toward me.

As his body flew, I tried to step out of his way, but it did no good. His long arms stretched out and he grabbed my waist, pulling me to his chest and flipping me over so that his back hit the floor. I fell on top of him with his hands cradling my head so my neck wouldn't twist.

His fingers dug into my hair and I gripped his shoulders as we stared at each other, gasping for breath and absorbing what had happened. It was like one of those movie moments where the couple leans in at a snail's pace and the audience just *knows* there will be a kiss.

He probably thought there would be a kiss, but before I stopped it— or allowed it—a voice broke through the din of the circus music. "What are you two doing? That is not appropriate behavior. Kids are watching!"

A chorus of "ooooohs" punctuated Mr. Bettencourt's rebuke. The kids were indeed watching.

Unbothered by Bettencourt's bad timing, Nico smirked as I pushed off his hard body. Was he made entirely of wood, because he sure felt like it? Being in his grasp like that, experiencing the feel of him underneath me had been intense.

But I was certain the flutter of my heart was due to the adrenaline, not him.

He popped up and put his hand on the small of my back as he guided me to where our boss was waiting. Mr. Bettencourt wasted no time laying into us. "I'm not surprised by your behavior Wood, but I'm appalled with yours, Miss Tyler. How could you allow yourself to get into that position? You're supposed to be turning him into a wholesome team player, not straddling him as soon as the lights dim."

"Mr. Bettencourt," I started, mainly to drown out the sound of Nico's snickers, but I didn't get any further than that.

"If you two are dating or hooking up or whatever they call it these days, stop immediately. There are clauses in both of your contracts to prevent this. If I find you in breach of it again, I'll have more than enough grounds to fire you both. Now, I must do what I can to smooth this over with my friend and these boys. You've done enough damage for one day. You should leave and reconsider how you conduct yourselves from this point forward."

After we'd taken off our gear and slinked back to the car—well, I slinked, Nico strutted—I made my best "I told you so" face. "To my knowledge members of the Flying Squirrels team, which is where you're likely to find yourself if you don't get it under control, don't have to actually become flying squirrels."

I'd been trying to make a point, but he turned it right around on me. "Really?" he smirked, grabbing his wooden fixture and smirking. "I have a Tower for my current team, so I just assumed…"

I groaned, throwing the car in gear and zooming out of the space. "At least I beat your ass today."

He threw his arm over the seat rest. "Nah. That's where you're wrong. I let you win."

Truth: Lines are Made to be ~~Crossed~~ Obliterated

Chapter 7
Nico

After a grueling, but good practice the next day, Laurel drove me all over San Antonio, dragging me to a series of photo ops and arguing that she'd beaten me fair and square at laser tag. She was captivating when she was riled up and I was pleased to learn our upcoming day consisted of a series of ask-no-questions-and-I'll-tell-no-lies scenarios. I smiled and high-fived and nodded myself into exhaustion. By the time she dropped me off, I was ready to eat and relax and think about how I'd stood still long enough for her to hit me with her laser before launching at her like I wanted to do again.

I was deep into that relaxation, lying on the couch in my gray boxer briefs flicking channels and sipping bourbon when my doorbell rang. Jumping up to grab my sweats, I peeked at the security camera and laughed my ass off.

No sweats necessary.

Swinging the door open, I leaned on the doorframe. "Hi, Shadow. What are you doing here at this hour?"

She looked different in her white tank top and ripped jeans. Her hair was in a mess on the top of her head that looked ripe for me to dig my hands into. And I couldn't help but notice that she wasn't wearing a bra.

Casual Laurel was next-level hot.

She took a lengthy look at my body, including the underwear, and swallowed. "I'm being spontaneous."

"By all means, come in for that," I drawled, stepping aside.

She marched into my living room and I followed her, amused that she was even there, much less discussing acts of spontaneity. "So, how are we going to be spontaneous tonight? Ladies choice."

Frowning, she put her hands on my shoulders, positioning me where she wanted me. Okay, I could work with that. "If you want to get it on right here in my living room, I'm good with it, but my bed's much bigger and more comfortable."

Gasping, she shook her head. "No. Not that," she sputtered, stepping around the coffee table and perching on the edge of the couch.

I chuckled. "Is this some kink you're trying to explain?"

"No. Shut up and listen. I was sitting at home getting ready for our day tomorrow, going over transcripts and prepping material for you when I realized maybe you'd been right about one thing. Maybe, I need to see it."

"See what?"

Her eye roll was epic. "You know what. It's not that I'm curious, I just think I need to know exactly what you have down there. I've heard what you've said about telling the truth and maybe there's a way…" Her cheeks were flushed the prettiest shade of pink. "I mean, to do my job to the best of my ability I need to have all the facts, no matter how awkward they may be."

I shrugged. "I don't feel awkward at all and I'm standing here in my underwear."

"I'm well aware you've got a serious lack of clothing happening over there."

"Glad you noticed. Now, why are you *really* here?"

I dared to take a step toward her, edging right up to the coffee table, but staying on my side. She took a deep breath like she had to work up to it. "Just let me see it. I'll look from over here and you'll stay there, then I'll leave. Nothing more. No lines crossed."

I wanted more than that. It felt like she did too, but I wasn't going to push it with her. Not until I knew for certain. Shrugging first, I hooked my thumbs into my waistband, pulled down my underwear, and stepped out of them, holding my arms wide. "Take as long as you want."

She tried desperately to hide her reaction, but I was studying her every move, her every breath, the way she scooted forward on the couch and squinted slightly.

That was pretty much all it took for that tingle to rise and make me harden for her. She didn't comment on my rising cock. She just sat as still as a boulder and stared at it.

And I stared at her staring at my cock.

Why was that so fucking hot? No idea.

After a few minutes, eyes flicked up. "Is that woodgrain? It's hard to tell from here."

There was the confirmation I was craving. She wanted a closer look, so a closer look she would have. I stepped over the coffee table, getting right in her face. She didn't budge. "Yes, it is. The skin covering it is mine, but wood is wood. The magic part is that it still feels like it should when you touch it." Her fists gripped the edge of the couch and I couldn't help but notice the way she began squirming and pressing her legs together.

"You can touch and see for yourself if you want."

Her tongue slicked over her bottom lip as her gaze shifted back to my wood. She was right there eye-level with it. All I had to do was lean forward and my cock would line up with her wet lips.

It nearly killed me to stand still.

She raised her hand, poised to do just that, but dropped it nanoseconds before she made contact. "I don't want to touch it."

"The hardened nipples poking through that snug shirt would say otherwise."

She crossed her arms over her chest. Too late. I'd already seen what I wanted to see and I was dizzy with the need to put the hard wood she was staring at right between her round breasts. Again, she whispered, "I don't want to touch it."

For a person not wanting to touch it, she sure was sitting right there inching toward it with the most excruciatingly slow crawl. "Shame. It certainly wants to touch you."

My need for her was too much to handle. I took my cock in my hand and met her halfway, running the tip over her lips for a brief moment—wanting to live in that gasp forever—before scoring it down her chin, the hollow of her throat, over the swell of one breast, then the other.

I went from hard to diamond wrapped in granite at the feeling of her.

Abandoning whatever internal rules had locked her away from this, from us, she arched toward me, closing her eyes as I tracked my cock across her chest, circling one of her peaks, then the other. The fabric of her shirt was between us, but with my extra sensitive dick, I was able to feel the pebbling of her skin as my cock teased her nipples.

Part of me couldn't believe she allowed it, but a bigger part of me knew she felt the same pull between us that I did.

I wasn't even inside her, but the way her mouth opened and the soft groans coming from her throat were so arousing, that I had to take more.

Wrapping one hand around the nape of her neck and pushing her against the back of the couch, I used my other hand to jerk her top down, exposing those luscious tits. This time, we both groaned as I ran my bare cock over her points.

She was as into it as I was, pulling my leg and helping me put one knee on the couch so I could get close enough to put my cock right between her breasts.

Thank fuck and Dr. Frankenpeen I'd waxed up before she'd arrived.

Maybe I should've asked or made sure she was okay with it, but when I began to thrust between her breasts, she threw her head back and gave me the fucking space to do it, so I let myself do what I wanted. What she wanted. "It feels so real," she whispered.

"It is real, Shadow. Real hard for your tits right now. Can't you feel this?" I grabbed her breasts between my hands, closing my shaft in with her sweet flesh as she squirmed against the couch. I wanted so much more of her but couldn't tear myself from her chest. It's like her tits were possessing me and keeping me there. "Unless you tell me to stop, I'm going to fuck your tits until I come."

She cracked an eye open, looking at me with dark dilated pupils. She smirked and when she didn't say stop, I was as turned on as I'd ever been. She seemed to like what I was doing, but I wanted more for her too. "Touch yourself. I want you to come too."

I could tell she was uneasy about that, but I distracted her by thumbing both nipples at the same time as I pressed her tits together. "What do you think of my wood cock?"

"I think it's…good. And…I see why you want to shout to the world about it. Don't stop. I've never…I like this a lot."

I laughed, still keeping up my pumping, enjoying the feel of her tits and when I looked down to watch her hand moving inside her jeans, it lit a fire inside me. She'd abandoned all pretense of professionalism, of boundaries—every line she'd ever drawn was left in the dust—and it was as beautiful as it was hot. "Fuck, this is so good," I muttered as my thrusting veered into out-of-control territory. It was potentially about to be that awkward moment she'd referred to earlier.

No sense in putting it off. I tilted her chin, forcing her to focus on my face. "I'm close now. Can I come on your tits?" I held my breath, knowing it may have crossed one of her invisible lines. While I wanted that more than I wanted anything, that may have been too much for two people who'd just met. I was prepared to turn to the side and obliterate my couch if necessary, but that's not what I hoped happened.

She nodded as her hips bucked against her hand. The sight and the permission she'd given was enough to bring me all the way home. The tingle started in my toes and worked its way through me. I pulled away from her and took my dick in my hand, holding it toward her chest as I exploded for her.

On her.

It was a sight to see my cum coating her perfect round breasts. Her shirt was probably ruined forever, but I'd buy her more. Hell, I'd give her my jersey with sixty-nine on it for allowing me this small window into her.

Watching as she fell apart too, I steadied myself for what could come after. She was too much of a thinker and thoughts can sometimes keep actions from appearing clear in the rearview.

She'd wanted this, but would she regret it tomorrow?

When her breathing was back to normal, I excused myself to go get a towel and a shirt for her to put on.

I was feeling pretty great about what had happened between us. Even better about her finally seeing the truth of what I had gone through and what I was now. We'd crossed a proverbial bridge in our relationship and I was already thinking of other fun things we could do next time.

Trotting back out with my supplies, I entered the living room, ready to give her a yes-yes list of those things, but I found myself alone.

She hadn't waited until tomorrow to regret it.

Cat Collins

54

#RegretsTasteLikeWhalies

Chapter 8
Laurel

I had no one to blame but myself.

Well, maybe I could blame some of it on the bottle of wine and my team members Jo and Joe. We'd been working on strategy for the team and for Nico when Joe mentioned how hot he was and Jo chimed in with ideas about how hard—no pun intended—it must be for him to have this foreign thing on his body replacing the one item most men prized the most.

Nico seemed to be fine with his new appendage, so I didn't feel sorry for him, but I felt something.

My mind had imagined all sorts of images when I thought about it and that was the problem: I thought about *it* too much. I couldn't focus on the job when I was constantly wondering and filling in the blanks. I needed to know, then I could move on from it. When I knew, I could dismiss it and him and be the professional I was hired to be.

Hoofing down his street and waiting for my Uber with the blanket I'd swiped from him to cover up his cum, I regretted my decision to sate my curiosity.

I was already teetering on the edge with him, liking how he poked at me, his sense of humor, and his looks, but I'd gotten a taste of him and I feared I would crave it again.

So unprofessional.

I climbed into the Uber, waving at the driver and hoping he'd understand I wasn't in the mood to talk. I had to think this thing through. I had to sort the facts from the feelings and try to stuff Nico back into the professional box I needed him to be in.

Fact: it looked like a regular cock, only prettier. If that was possible. Something about the woodgrain and the way it blended and complimented his already stellar body was like he'd been painted by a master artist. Although, I guessed all art is subjective, so I filed that under feelings, and not facts.

Fact: his new wooden cock felt like a normal cock, only better. The skin was soft and warm, but the wooden core made it feel harder than a normal aroused dick. As soon as he touched my lips with his tip, my stomach tightened and I couldn't keep from wiggling to relieve the throbbing in my core. He'd turned me on and it was nearly instant, so I guessed that one fell under feeling instead of fact too.

Fact: it functioned like a dick should. When he came, I came right with him. It was so hot and dirty, what he'd done, but so intense and the connection it created between us still hummed in my mind and body.

I sighed, burrowing into his blanket. I was finding it impossible to separate facts from feelings.

I was in deep trouble with him. Down to the depths of the ocean, trouble. I had to get over these feelings and get back to professional mode before I saw him again.

I just wished I knew how.

The next morning, he climbed in the car, chipper as ever and looking like he'd gone the extra mile on his appearance wearing tight jeans that hugged his crotch and a gray V-neck, a smattering of chest hair peeking out and drawing all eyes to his defined pecs. Damn him.

I braced myself for his comments.

"Good morning, Shadow. Did you suddenly remember you had a meeting with the President last night or something equally important?"

"Listen, I—"

"Nope. You listen. What happened last night was incredible. I suspect you ran away from me because you assumed we crossed some invisible line or you thought it wouldn't trend right for us to hook up. Well, you can forget that nonsense. We are consenting adults and fuck me, if that wasn't the hottest thing I've ever done. I intend to do it again and then some."

"But we can't."

"Bullshit."

"Nico, you know Mr. Bettencourt told us. He would have a fit if he knew."

"I don't plan on telling him, do you?"

"No, but I can't risk this. He's very important in this community and his moral compass points way far away from what we did last night. If we were discovered and he fired us, his influence would keep me from getting any other jobs in this city." Nico smirked, a very odd reaction to what I was saying. "Why are you grinning?"

He slid his arm over my seat, turning toward me and getting close enough that I could smell his intoxicating scent. "Because, Shadow, you just confirmed that you've thought about it. You probably went home and made a list of all the reasons why we can't be together, right? Well, that just means you're trying to talk yourself out of it ergo, you want me."

I hated how easy it was for him to peg me.

God, *peg me*? I was sounding dirty to myself.

I opened my mouth to argue with him, to deny it, but he put his finger over my lips. "Sh. It's okay. Make all the lists you want. I know the truth now. And let me be clear, I have a list too; a list of all the sexy, dirty, mind-blowing things I'm going to do to that banging body of yours. If you think last night was good, you just wait until my magic wand gets a hold of you next." His declaration said, he reached around and buckled my seatbelt before doing his own. "Where are we going today?"

When I said deep trouble, what I meant was the unfathomable depths of the Mariana Trench.

I slammed the car in gear, backing out of his drive and nearly hitting his mailbox as I sped onto the street. "Add magic wand to the list."

The toothpaste endorsement had gone well the day before, so I buried visions of what had happened between us deep in my brain and carted him across town to the Tower fan meeting. A group got together every week before a game and sometimes B-players or staff would show up and speak with them. Nico had never been before because he was just too high up the Tower food chain to bother, but my goal was to make him like the every-man and they'd leave singing his praises. He was great with people and I believed he could do it and come out unscathed.

"Remember, no talk of your wood, family-friendly, focus on the game or your stats, use the same charm you did with the moms and kids at the toothpaste event."

"And you, of course," he smiled, then he saluted me and strutted in the restaurant like he owned the place. He did that with every room he entered. It was annoying. And a little hot.

A hushed silence fell over the group when they noticed him. He strolled over to the buffet and helped himself to a plate, nodding and talking with the staff while the rest of the Tower fans sat with their mouths hanging open.

The guy who looked like the president of the club went over and welcomed him, telling him to sit at the front table, but before he did so, he sauntered to the back of the room where I'd perched and handed me the plate he'd just made before fixing himself another and taking his place.

If he was trying to look good in front of the fans, that scored him major points with the ladies in the room.

And me.

Nope, I wasn't keeping score.

Do your job, Laurel. Nothing more.

No matter how sexy it was that he fixed your plate for you.

Trouble.

After the meal, he took questions. The first ones were game-centered where he talked strategy and logistics. Then one old guy in the back of the room stood, placing his weight on an ancient hockey stick he was using for a cane. "So, what's the deal with your cock, Wood?"

Murmurs broke out across all the tables as Nico ran his hands over his jeans. He didn't look uncomfortable, not really, but I knew he was having trouble with the lying I'd forced on him. "Hey John, it's good to see you again. To answer your question, I'll just say the deal with my cock is the same as the deal as yours. Nothing special, I'm afraid, but don't tell the ladies."

Laughter.

That was good.

"Come on, I've been supporting the Tower for fifty years, and ever since you've been on this team, you've been the most forthright player I've seen. I know you won't bullshit us with a corporate message. There's got to be some truth to what you said about it. Cold medicine, my ass."

The group was silent. Nico glanced at me and I felt the "*I told you so*" in his gaze. He took a deep breath to steel himself. "It's like this. I'd love to be able to say I had a magical penis, but sometimes the truth is stranger than fiction. Not all meds mix and I was off my head when I spoke that day. You can see I'm well and ready to play this weekend though, so you come on out and support the team. I'd love to see you all there!"

He waved as he exited the room, his anger emanating from him. As soon as we hit the door, he spun around. "I don't like lying."

"I know. It's for the best though."

"For you maybe."

"For you, Nico. You don't want to get fired."

He huffed in frustration, throwing himself back in the car. "What's next on my tour of deceit?"

We made three more stops.

The first was at a gas station where Nico pumped gas for people. I'd thought that was a great idea, but the first time he said the word 'pump' it sounded so dirty, that I shut it off after thirty minutes.

My car was starting to become an argument zone. "I didn't mean it like that. I said, 'Let me pump your gas for you,' just like you told me. I can't help it if the woman snickered and handed me her number. I can only control myself, Laurel."

"It doesn't seem like you're doing that. Just forget it. Add pump to the list."

He huffed. "Not enough paper in the world to add all your no-no words."

"Um, the list was on the phone. No paper required."

In the silence on the way to the next location, I realized he might have been right. The woman had reacted to a simple sentence. Maybe I'd been too hasty in shutting it down, but I didn't want to hear any other women doing the same thing. It would steer things right back to the subject I was trying to avoid in two capacities: his amazing dick.

The next stop would be better. I was sure of it.

I veered into the bookstore, checking my phone for messages from Jo and Joe. They were handling the brunt of the social media postings while I was handling Nico. They'd set this one up for me though, so we were both going in blind.

"Okay, you are signing copies of the latest Stix hockey magazine. That's it."

"Oh, you mean the one with me on the cover that says I'm the number one player in the league?"

"You knew I meant that one."

"I did. It was fun to remind you."

I shoved him forward and he looked over his shoulder. "I'm into how rough and handsy you are."

"That's what I'm talking about. None of that. Go."

I pulled a bottle of water from my bag, downing it in one gulp. He'd unnerved me with that one. He wasn't talking to any fans or press. He was talking to me and getting more and more familiar as he did so.

Letting him get close had been a colossal mistake. I hated myself for not respecting my own boundaries. He was just so…irresistible.

Fifteen minutes later, came the first fan wearing a t-shirt with the Tower logo that had been changed into a penis with a bulbous head on top. Some idiot college guy. He was really proud of himself. "Yo, dude. How do you get to Dr. Frankenpeen? I need some new game."

Nico laughed and I threatened him with laser beam eyes that told him to behave. He righted himself after he huffed a good thirty seconds. "Figment of my cold-med imagination, I'm afraid. No such guy exists, but wouldn't it be cool if there was?"

He uncapped the sharpie, prepping to sign the shirt, but I ripped it out of his hand. "No. Don't."

The college kid groaned. "Come on, it's funny. Let him sign it."

I grabbed Nico's ear and pulled him away from the table. Was I losing my cool? Maybe. As soon as I had him behind a bookshelf, he grinned. "You do enjoy touching my person, don't you? It's just a little walk down to where you know you want to go. You know I wouldn't stop you."

I growled. He wiggled his eyebrows. "Do that again."

"Stop. You cannot sign a penis-shaped Tower shirt. Mr. Bettencourt will go ballistic. Let's just get out of here and go… I don't know where."

He crossed his arms and leaned back against the bookshelf, jutting his pelvis forward. The quintessential hot-guy pose. "You seem flustered, Shadow. How can I help?"

The back of my neck prickled with heat. "You can help by doing what I say. Get rid of the kid and go back to the approved script."

I had to get away from him, so I sped out of the door and back to the haven of my car. An hour later, he strolled out of the bookstore with an armful of books and a big smile. He handed me the books as he slid into the seat. "These are for you."

I flipped through the titles, all of them self-help books about being honest or finding yourself, and there was one on Social Media too. "You enjoy mocking me, don't you?"

He shrugged. "A little."

This time when I put the car in gear, I ran over the curb to get to the main road.

Truth: The Truth is Always Simpler

Chapter 9
Nico

Watching Laurel stew made me hard.

She'd probably say there was something wrong with me for that, but I failed to care. Getting under her skin was the step before getting under her, period.

I gave her some thinking space as she brought me home. I enjoyed affecting her like that. She was smart and very good at her job, but that spark she tried to drown in herself was what I was after.

Grabbing my stuff first, I leaned back in the window. She was already on her phone scrolling. "Oh my word, Nico, what did you do?"

At first, I wasn't sure what she was talking about this time, but it came back to me. I'd bought some of those naughty books women raved about on social media and handed them out in the bookstore. I looked at it as a nice gesture, but she didn't see it that way. "Hashtag, WoodGaveItToMe is trending!"

"Hm? I don't see how twenty women could trend anything."

"You don't understand social media or women, do you? It's not about the twenty women you bought books for, it's about the thousands of others who want people to believe they were one of them."

Okay, fair enough. I still didn't see the problem. Moreover, neither did she. "I do understand women, you know. I understand that you are doing things you don't want to do just because some old cereal tycoon with a hard-on for hockey is telling you to. You should come out of your comfort zone and play with me, Laurel. There would be no end to the clever things you could devise if you leaned into the wood cock thing. Deep down, you know you'd love it. We've seen that firsthand."

For a moment, she looked like she was going to say something, but she drove away in silence to think. Which left me alone to do the same.

63

The first thing that popped into my mind was how I would love to show her exactly what my wood cock could do when I got inside her. I got so hard over it, that I went straight upstairs for my wax.

I spent the following two days doing phone interviews, towing the party line about Dr. Frankenpeen and the woodpecker in my pants.

Laurel still rode my ass over every word out of my mouth and refused to ride my cock, no matter how often I reminded her how amazing our time together had been.

The longer we went like this, the harder I was for this woman. Even more interesting was that my special wooden pal was growing.

Literally.

I wasn't sure at first, but I got out the tape measure to be certain. I'd been upset that the length and girth of the thing hadn't been up to my former glory, but it was way beyond that now. I was huge and hard. All the fucking time.

I wanted to excuse myself and jerk off every chance I got, but I was determined to hang on, hard and horny, doing as I was told until she stopped feeding me the 'we're keeping it professional' line.

On Sunday—game day—I faced the same crowd of reporters that had caused me to go off the rails before, including Hunter Cato and the ESPN correspondent.

Laurel escorted me from the car, reminding me of all the things I wasn't supposed to say. When we were feet away, she swung me around, looking up into my eyes. "One more thing. Can you please put that away?"

"Put what away?"

Her eyes darted down. "That. You cannot walk over there with a bulge in your pants like that. Think of your grandma having sex with a horse or something equally unappealing. Get that monster back in the cage."

I looked down. "Thanks for that visual, but I can't help you, Shadow. It's not like I'm trying to show off. You could always help me out," I offered. "Maybe my cock's growing because I want you so bad and you keep reminding me how professional you are."

She licked her lip. "That's ridiculous. Don't ever wear those pants again. Here." She shoved my duffle bag at me. "Hold it in front of you."

She pushed me toward the reporters, but I turned back. "So nice of you to notice Mr. Happy. He'd really like another chance to get to know you."

Growling, she left me and took her place at the back of the crowd so it didn't look like I was being coached, even though I was.

She was wearing a white V-neck tee under her Tower blue blazer, and a flowy gray skirt that made her ass look phenomenal. Our team colors never looked so good. It was difficult for me to even find a reporter to talk with because my gaze kept falling on her.

I managed to focus when the ESPN guy shoved the mic at me. "How are you feeling today, Nico?"

"Ready and willing to take the Blackhawks down. The team is at one hundred percent and we're going to show the Hawks not to mess with us."

Game-focused question and good response. All on track.

"You've been involved with some interesting projects this week. Any truth to the rumors that you're trying to save your job because of your outrageous claims regarding your manhood have got you on the chopping block?"

Panic washed over Laurel's face. I wanted to go over and comfort her and tell her I had it, but of course, I couldn't. "Listen, Steve. Is your name Steve? You seem like a Steve. Every hockey player's job is on the line. If we don't play well, we're out. That's the way it's always been in the NHL.

"Yeah, I did some press and charity events this week because I'm proud to be leading the Tower and I love our supporters. If you'll go back and read all the transcripts, I have set the record straight on my original outlandish claims about my manhood multiple times." I used air quotes. It hurt a little because it seemed like I was saying I didn't have a dick at all, but I carried on. Laurel was about to puke on her shoes.

"I have the manhood I was born with and I am now off the cold medicine. Docs have cleared me for this game. Now if you'll excuse me, I'm going to go prepare. Thanks for your time."

The lies were starting to taste like bile.

I said them for Laurel, but I was getting close to my dishonesty threshold. It all seemed way out of hand. The truth is always simpler.

Hoping it would all be over once I wiped the Blackhawks off the ice, I went to the locker room to change into my gear, which proved to be harder than I ever imagined it would be.

After he'd watched Ted Lasso a hundred times, Coach Anthony started implementing these pregame rituals that were utterly mental. So far, he'd made us do pushups before we spoke, leave the spectators notes in the stands, and once we had to sing everything we said like we were in a damned Broadway show. We'd complained the whole time but the team started leaning into them when our winning streak increased.

Coach would change tactics after a loss and I'll be damned if we didn't have a winning streak for at least ten or twelve games after we got a new ritual to try.

His current pregame ritual was making the team get dressed two hours before necessary and not speaking to each other until the game started. Wacky as shit, but it had worked for the team while I was away, so who was I to doubt it?

Not wanting to buck the system and accidentally speak, most of the players filtered around to different spots in the locker room or somewhere else in the player-only part of the building.

I wandered down the hall, looking for a very private space because I had a big problem.

And by big, I mean huge.

As I'd started to gear up, I realized my compression shorts with built-in cup weren't fitting anymore.

I couldn't stuff my prick inside.

Nothing I did worked. I tried some creative cramming, some rearranging down there and even considered going jock-less. I was told my wood was durable, but as I fiddled around trying to make it work, I realized that even though it was wood, I couldn't skate around with it hanging out like that.

This was more than an inconvenience. It was screwing with my game. I had to get through a match without another cocktastrophe. Laurel would be furious if I went out on this ice in this state. And while I loved it when she got all flustered, I wasn't keen on pissing her off.

I ended up sneaking into the film room. It was empty and had a lock on it, which I took advantage of right away, so nobody could come in and hear the phone call I was about to make. Again, Laurel would've killed me if someone had overheard.

I got out my phone and scrolled until I found the contact I had listed under 'Cock Doc.'

He answered on the second ring. "Dr. Frankenpeen, what's up?" He devolved into a laughing fit, amused by his own joke. "Get it? What's *up*? This is the penises I am referring to."

I wasn't laughing.

"Hey Frankenpeen, it's Nico Wood. I have an issue. My wooden cock seems to have grown exponentially over the past week. Is that normal?"

"No, I wouldn't say it this is normal."

Great. "Am I malfunctioning then, because I can't stuff this thing into my jock at the moment."

"Not necessarily a malfunction. What do you think has caused this growth?"

I thought back to when it started and came up with one answer. Specifically, one person. "I'm very attracted to this woman I've been spending time with. She makes me as hard as she makes me angry sometimes. I mean, I just want to take her and—"

"Nope. This is not your issue."

"Okay, then what is it?"

"You have been given the penis made from the magic puppet. The growth occurs when you stretch the truth, as was the problem with the puppet."

His German accent was thick, so I wasn't sure if I was hearing him right. "You are saying that when I lie, my member grows?"

"Dah."

All the oxygen seemed to whose from my lungs. This couldn't be true. "Everyone lies, Doc."

"Dah, of that I'm sure, however you must not. Simple. Problem solved."

Spots formed around the edges of my vision. "I have to lie to save my job."

"Zen your only other recourse is sex. You must ejaculate yourself to rid the body of the lies. Once you do, your penal size shall restore to the factory settings, so to speak."

I was certain my head was going to explode.

Literally and figuratively.

"Why didn't you tell me about this when I was with you? It's crucial information," I bellowed into the phone.

"I didn't? I was certain I must have. Ah well, at least you know now. I must go. I have another re-membering transplant waiting for me. Tschuss!"

Wow. Okay. I needed to fuck the lies out of me. It was crazy, but I didn't hate the idea of it, though I did want to punch Frankenpeen for failing to tell me in the first place.

Didn't have that luxury at the moment, so I tried to put those feelings aside. I dug my wax out of the bag and went into the bathroom adjacent to the film room. Within moments I was waxed and pumping, picturing Laurel and what we'd done together as I tried to solve my problem and give myself a little feelgood action and flush the lies out.

It didn't work.

I couldn't do it.

This had never—and I mean never—happened before.

It was like my shaft was *too* hard to function.

My mind was under too much pressure: Lie, save your job, win the game, lie some more, don't kill Foxx, lie again, Laurel putting the brakes on, don't be angry with the doc.

It was too much. I was so in my head that I couldn't jerk off.

It was insane. I had a raging hard-on, but I could get it up at the same time.

I pulled up my pants and slinked into one of the seats with my phone in my hand, trying to wrap my head around my new problem.

I was pissed that I wasn't given the information before I left and I was even angrier that I couldn't rub one out to save myself.

I had to find a way out of this or I was a goner. Checking the time first—one hour before warmups—I pulled up another number.

"Where are you? You're supposed to be available for photoshoots if I need you."

"Hey, Shadow. I'm in the film room. You need to come right away."

Little white lie. *I* needed to come right away.

#LyingMakesYouHorny

Chapter 10
Laurel

I found Nico leaning against the wall outside the film room, waiting for me. He had that hot-guy smirk on his face and I could see in his eyes that he was up to something.

I slowed as I reached him. "What's so important? I need to vet the people for the meet and greet."

He gestured, flicking his eyes downward. I almost swallowed my tongue. Had he grown larger?

No. That was stupid. It was just a trick of his sweatpants.

I tore my gaze off the bulge, looking up at him. "What's going on?"

He kicked off the wall. "I'm going to be honest with you. My wooden dick came with a condition I knew nothing about until now. Every time I tell a lie, it grows."

"We don't have time for games now, Nico."

"Trust me, this isn't a game. It's my life. When I lie, my dick grows, just like the puppet whose wood I'm now sporting. I thought the growth, the hardness I was feeling was just an attraction to you."

He'd made himself clear on that point over and over, but I'd pushed him away, keeping it professional for both of us. It was hard because there was so much about him I liked. We couldn't though. We worked together and our contracts specifically forbade it.

He continued, "Dr. Frankenpeen confirmed that the lies I've been telling have caused my shaft to enlarge out of my jockstrap, which kinda sucks on game day."

That sounded painful. And dangerous for a hockey player.

"So, what do you do? Get a larger jock?"

"I already have the biggest one, thanks." He put his hands on my waist, turning me around and backing me against the wall. "Bigger equipment won't work. The only thing that will is sex."

It was his big game day and he was acting ridiculous. "You're shitting me."

"I'm not and I'll prove it." He took my hand and placed it on his cock. It was over the sweats, but I could still make out the hard ridges. My mouth watered even though I tried to force myself not to react.

"When I lie, it grows." Nico looked down through his lashes. "Did you feel anything just then?"

I kept staring at my hand on his crotch. It was taking everything in me not to rub. Oh, I wanted to rub, but I couldn't. Touching him like that was not okay, but in this case, I needed to know. That's what I told myself anyway. I nodded in the negative. "I just feel your abnormally large wooden peen."

He took a step forward, holding my hand in place over his cock, then using his other one and his body to pin me against the wall. "Pay attention: I think you're an unattractive, bothersome, unpleasant woman and I don't want to fuck you. In fact, I wouldn't have sex with you if you were the last woman on earth."

I released a shuddering breath as the hardness beneath my hand grew. He moaned as I stretched my fingers apart to touch the farthest reaches of the defined ridges.

It had grown.

I looked up at him, realizing the lies he'd told to produce the growth. He wanted me as much as I wanted him, but we couldn't cross that line. "You're my client."

"No. Bettencourt is your client. I'm just a guy whose dick you're fondling."

Was I?

I looked down.

Yep.

I tried to remove my hand, but he stopped me. To further prove his point, he guided my hand, up and down his member as he raised his hips.

My stomach was coiled with that delicious heat that made me want to…do things. His cock did feel good.

But we couldn't. "So go jerk off and take care of it."

"Tried. Can't. I need you to help me, Laurel."

"Nico," I whispered, unsure of where the sentence was going.

"I see your mind turning. You're weighing the consequences, thinking of how it would look, doing damage control before the damage. Don't do that. Don't think. Just act. For once, do what you want to do, not what's expected."

There was a pleading in his voice that made my insides melt.

Still.

"We shouldn't. Maybe you should excuse yourself from the game."

"Never going to happen."

Somehow I tore myself out of his grip, wishing I'd stayed where I was, hating how I'd let the chance to be with him go.

It was the right thing to do. I couldn't lose another job over a man.

He shrugged, his eyes going from molten to cold in a heartbeat. "Fine, I'd never force you or any woman to do what you didn't want." He turned to go down the hall away from me, not even glancing back.

I called out. "Wait. Where are you going?"

"To find a puck bunny to help me out. I need a fast and dirty fuck and if you're not interested, I can find a dozen women within a stone's throw who are."

My stomach clenched. For a couple of reasons.

"You can't trust that a puck bunny will keep her mouth shut about your cock. It's too risky."

He chuckled, turning around and marching back toward me. "Is it too risky or are you jealous?"

Both.

"It's not that."

"Yeah, it is."

This time he grabbed both wrists, pinning them above my head against the film room door. "That's the truth for free. And here's another fact for you, Shadow. Maybe my dick is a magic lie detector, but that's not the only thing going on here.

"You make me hard and I've done nothing but think of ways to please you since the first time I laid eyes on you. Every time you use that smart mouth on me I want to shut it up with a kiss. Don't let your head get in the way of what I can promise you will make your body beg for more of me."

I opened my mouth, but none of the rational arguments I wanted to give came out. Instead, I said, "Okay."

It was the permission he needed, so he slammed his lips against mine with a force so brutal it took my breath away.

I matched that force, trying to get my arms down, but failing as he leaned against me with that immaculate body and held me where he wanted. A battle formed in our lips and tongues as we kissed, nibbled, nipped at each other, moaning and giving into the heat between us.

It was hot. And a little dirty. And I couldn't believe how well we fit as we found a rhythm together, going from rough to soft lingering kisses that made the desire inside me crest like a wave.

This man knew what he was doing. He drew me out myself as if I were in the middle of an out-of-body experience.

He fumbled with the door for a second, but never stopped kissing, shoving me inside and locking it behind us. He slammed his hand against some buttons on the wall to make the film play. Finally pulling away to say, "I've thought too much about this to not want to see every move of your body and every expression you make as I pump you with this hard wooden cock."

Good grief. I almost spontaneously combusted at his words, but he wasn't done. "Is that what you want, Shadow? Do you want this magic wood inside you?"

I nodded. "Yeah, I don't want to lie about this anymore."

~Nico~

I dropped my pants as fast as humanly possible. This was the dream and I was living it. Confirming she wanted me was just as exciting as being able to get back in my jock later. She'd done more than permit me to fuck her, she'd allowed a window for us to experiment in a way I couldn't wait to try.

But we had to work up to that.

Pressing her against the wall, I kissed her gently. Yeah, I liked the hard bruising kisses, but her mouth was soft and pliable and I loved the way we kissed each other with matching fire. I also loved the way she clung to me like she needed me to hold her up.

I could do that.

After I'd kissed her breathlessly, I dropped to my knees, eager to kiss her other places. Her dark eyes tracked my hands as I traced her legs, raising her skirt in the process.

Not wanting to take the slow route—this time anyway—I stuck my finger inside her panties, pulling them aside to give me room. She gasped as I raked my tongue over her clit. It was already pulsing with need and when I sucked on it, her hips bucked forward. "Oh yeah. Do that."

I hummed, flicking my tongue over her slit. "Always telling me what to do."

"Yes, now do it. Suck my clit again."

"Yes, ma'am," I murmured against her. I liked this side of her. The one who'd lost all her control. "Is this what you want?"

Sucking harder, I pressed a finger into her wetness. Oh, this woman has turned the fuck on. I added a second finger, pumping in and out as I sucked, growing harder with every moan and thrust. She gripped my hair. "This feels so incredible."

I managed to look up. Her head was thrown back, her chest heaving. She was close to coming, but I wasn't going to let her go off the cliff that easily. I wanted to edge her into oblivion.

I slowed my pumping fingers and fluttered my tongue over the tip of her clit, giving her a different sensation that she ate up. Her legs started trembling, so I knew I was giving it to her good. If I could have, I would have slowed my roll and kept it up for hours, but this time I had to be more mission-oriented with this.

Pulling myself up, I kissed her temple. "Now that you're ready for it, do you want to see how big your lies have made me?

She nodded, biting her lower lip before she reached out and pulled down my sweatpants. She raised an eyebrow before she twisted me in the direction of the screen still playing silent game highlights. "Good grief. It's a monolith."

I cocked my head. "Yep, and it is all yours for the taking. This time, I'm not going to settle for just your tits though. I want that pussy."

When she reached out to run her fingers over my shaft, I shuddered. Her touch was light and it sent feathers of warmth through my body. While I wished she could stay right there on her knees, I knew I had to make it fast. Time was ticking on the game and we'd have more of it to do all sorts of things later. So, I pulled her over to the back row of seats. "Knees on the chair. Hands on the back."

She pushed me away playfully, but then got right in the position for me like a good fucking girl. "Like this?" I couldn't have scripted it better if I tried. It was like she was inside my head living out my every fantasy.

"Yeah. Just like that. Let me see that beautiful ass."

I pulled her skirt up over her back and got a good look at the thong she wore and her exceptional round ass. I would be doing all sorts of things to it later, but again, I needed release, so I pulled down her panties to reveal her glistening pussy. "This is going to be fun," I said as I rubbed the tip of my cock across her wetness.

She peeked over her shoulder with a sexy smirk, fully into this. "Yeah, but maybe next time try a lie."

I chuckled as the heady scent of her reached my nose. Naughty girl.

My chest was pounding and I was starting to see spots I was so horny for her, so I pushed inside, enjoying the warmth as my cock sank into her depths. We moaned our pleasure together.

She felt so good I could've stayed inside her forever, but that dirty girl started moving, pulling forward, and squeezing my dick in the process, telling me she wanted me to give it to her good, so I did. I stepped forward, pumping and thrusting, easy at first, but when her groans came out in a steady rhythm, I picked up my pace, slamming into her with more abandon. "That's good, just like I—" Wait a second. That wasn't going to work.

I started again, "This feels like shit. Your pussy is a desert."

We both gasped as my cock expanded. Being inside her like that as I grew? It sent a tremor through my whole body, along with the tingling heat. The feeling was intense for me. For her too by the sound of it. "Lie again," she grunted as I railed her nearly uncontrollably.

"This will be the last time we do this."

Bigger.

Harder.

Faster, we went.

"I'm never going to take you like this again. We are terrible together and you suck."

She raised so her back was flush with my chest, giving us a new angle and sensation altogether. I changed my motions, thrusting up as I held her with one hand. The other I snaked around to the front and began playing with that swollen clit. All the while she panted my name and moaned her pleasure.

"This was the worst idea ever."

This time her moan was more of a grunt and a squeal. "I don't know if I can take any more lies."

"Sure, you can. Let me stretch you out, Shadow. Your pussy's no good."

I was nearly blind with desire for her and I was getting close to losing it, so I released her hip and grabbed the length of her hair, wrapping it around my fist and pulling her back. "Lean back. I want to kiss you when we come." One-hundred percent truth there.

She reached behind, grabbed for me, and laid her head back so we could kiss. The slight change of positions made us both moan again. I thrust inside her, loving how her soft walls clenched my wood so well that I could no longer hold on.

I pinched her clit as my balls swelled. "Do you feel that? Come with me, Shadow. Let me feel it." She cried out as I spilled inside her. It went on forever and she rode it out with me, squeezing as hard as she could to wring all the pleasure from us both.

And I felt every tense muscle, every slick of my cock, each heaving beat of her heart against my chest as we finished.

When it was done, I pressed a soft kiss to her neck as she cooed like a baby and tried to breathe normally. We stayed that way for a while. I would've preferred a much longer afterglow session, but we didn't have the luxury of time, so I pulled out and checked my size, simultaneously happy and deflated about it. "Back to normal. I suppose I should say thank you."

She giggled. The sound echoed through the room and found its way inside me. Hearing her with her walls fully dropped was amazing. I liked her like this, unfettered and unrestrained. "You're welcome, I suppose. Now, I have a question I've been wondering since the first time. What's inside me, cum or sap?"

Cat Collins

Lie: Your Boss Can't Fire You For Fucking In a Car

Chapter 11
Nico

My extremely good mood helped us put another one in the W column. It wasn't just me though, the whole team was on fire as we gave it to the Blackhawks and sent them packing with a three-point deficit.

It was good to be back on the ice.

It was good just to be alive.

Corny as it sounded, fucking Laurel had been phenomenal and I was a dozen different kinds of excited about it. She was like a dream come to life and I wanted to explore more with her. As I changed into my gray pin-striped suit for the after-party, I couldn't stop thinking about it happening again. I was conjuring all sorts of lies to say when I was inside her soft depths once more.

I was in such a good mood, I didn't even blink when Foxx threw his phone at me. He'd just gotten off a phone call and was pissed beyond reason. He chucked his phone across the locker room and it sailed right for my crotch. I was quick to turn, so it just grazed me. I picked it up and handed it back to him. "Be careful. It would probably cost you more to replace your phone than me to replace my dick again." I slapped his back. "See ya at the party."

The team always rented out one of the swanky restaurants on the River Walk after every game and another one of Coach Anthony's Ted Lasso-inspired requirements was that all players attend for at least an hour. I usually stayed long enough to pick up a puck bunny, but I had someone else on my mind.

The party was already in full swing when I arrived. Navigating the crowd of teammates and fans who all wanted high fives or hugs or to congratulate me was difficult, but I finally made it to the bar and got a Moscow mule to sip as I scanned the crowd for Laurel.

My mood plummeted when I couldn't find her. I know I told her I was coming, but it occurred to me that I hadn't invited her in so many words. She was supposed to be my shadow, so she should've been lurking somewhere.

Unless she was going down that awful road of regret again.

Downing my drink, then grabbing another, I pulled out my phone to check for messages from her. When I found none, I shot her a text, asking her to come find me by the bar. I had to admit I experienced a rare case of jitters as I waited for her to show up. I wasn't the kind of guy who waited around for women so that was new territory for me. I didn't much care for it.

I leaned against the bar, my eyes never stopping their sweep of the room. "Hey, Nico. Great game tonight. You looked amazing on the ice and in that suit too."

Turning to see who was interrupting my surveillance, I found a blonde puck bunny named Cassie, no, Casey, or maybe Kelsey, hell, I couldn't remember. We'd hooked up a few times in the past. I raised my glass to her. "Thanks.

She wrapped her small hand around my bicep. "Can we get a selfie? We didn't take one last time."

"Uh, sure," I mumbled as she cozied up to me with her phone in one hand. I tried to lean away from her so it wouldn't be so intimate, but she wasn't having that. She clung to me like she was a baby and I was her mother's tit.

I flashed a smile for the camera and held up a finger to make it look like I was doing a 'We're Number One' gesture, thinking it would make the photo look like a fan thing and not a 'we're hooking up thing' like she wanted.

Shit. Laurel had me thinking with a social media mind now. Go figure.

After the photo was done and posted to Instaface or whatever media site, she moved her hand to my chest, rubbing and mentally undressing me with her eyes. "Whatever training you did during your injury paid off. I bet you're even more jacked than you were before."

I nodded politely. "Yeah, I guess maybe."

"I'd love to see it in person. If you recall, we had a lot of fun last time," she offered, licking her lips and looking at me like I was her next meal.

Any other night, I might have taken her up on it.

"Hey, I'd love to chat more, but I need to go take care of something. It was great seeing you again."

My cock grew a couple of inches at least on that one. Three lies, boom, boom, boom. Her face fell. "Okay then. I'll be around if you change your mind later." She got up on her toes to kiss my cheek, just as my eyes connected with Laurel's across the room.

She'd just walked in the door in a sexy sapphire halter dress that clung to her curves. She'd left her hair down and it fell in bouncy waves around her shoulders. My mouth dried at the sight of her.

Her mouth, however, hung open at the sight of Cassie/Casey/Kelsey hanging all over me and kissing the fuck out of my cheek while trying to get me to turn and really kiss her.

Shit.

Laurel spun on her heel and went right back out the door.

Shit. Shit. Shit.

I peeled the blonde off, not even bothering to apologize or say goodbye, and then I tore off across the room and out the door, catching up with Laurel as she reached her car. "Hey, where are you going?"

She froze, not even turning around. "Um, you don't need me here tonight. I'm tired, so I'm just going to take off."

I stepped up to her, running my hands over her bare shoulders. "But you look stunning. Why not come in and let everyone see how hot you are?"

"Oh, thanks. I don't know...I just..." I kissed her shoulder and she winced.

Not what I wanted.

"Turn around Laurel."

"I'm just going to go. See you tomorrow."

She went to open the door, but I put my hand on the handle so she couldn't. "Turn around."

Slowly, and I mean *slowly*, she turned to face me, though she didn't look up. I put my finger under her chin and made her. Her dark eyes searched mine, looking for something. "Are we going to do the jealousy thing, because that woman in there was throwing everything at me, but I wasn't catching."

She slicked her tongue over her lower lip. My cock sprung to attention. "I'm not jealous. I just realized we shouldn't have had sex earlier. It was bad enough the first time we... We can't do it again, Nico. It's unprofessional and I can't take the risk. The next time find someone else to help you out with your enlarging problem."

I leaned in close to her ear, licking the shell of it before I whispered into it. "I *do* think you're jealous and I don't want anyone else. What do you say to that?"

She tried to step away, but I pinned her against the car with my arms. "I don't have anything to say other than we need to keep it professional."

"Hm. Well," I skated one finger over her shoulder, across her collarbone, over the swell of her breasts that were peeping out of that dress. She didn't move an inch to stop me. "I say fuck professionalism. I'm glad you're jealous of some nameless puck bunny. It means you want me too, so we're going to walk over to the passenger side of this car, I'm going to get in, let the seat back, then you're going to climb on top of me and feel this hard cock from a different direction. Sound good?"

She opened her mouth. "I don't—" I put my finger over it. "If your next sentence isn't I don't want to wait any longer, then you're the liar here." She whimpered against my finger. "That's what I thought. Come on." I took her by the hand and did exactly what I promised to do by climbing in, moving the seat, and then undoing my fly and pulling my pants and underwear down so she could hop on.

I was half-mast before, but I grabbed the wax I'd stashed in her car, slathering it over my dick and rubbing it as I looked up at her. "That dress is perfect, but I'm going to wrinkle the shit out of it in one minute." She watched my hand pump up and down my shaft, her gaze turning ravenous. "You like watching me rub my cock like this?"

She nodded, biting her lip. "Mm-hm."

"Every time I touch myself I think about you."

Her response was to pull up the skirt of her dress and climb on top of me. "I think about you too. I tried to stop myself, but I can't seem to get you out of my head."

"That's right where I want to be, Shadow." I kissed her softly, hoping I was conveying something more than just sex in the kiss. I liked this woman. I wanted to be around her, wanted to make her laugh, to make her moan. "I want to be right here too." I shifted my pelvis, running it against her pussy as I reached behind her neck, undoing the tie that held her halter in place. She gasped as I leaned down, taking a nipple in my mouth and grabbing the other with my hand.

Her tits were perfect, round, and bouncy, and her nipple responded by hardening under my tongue. I switched to the other side, just to feel it again. She threw her head back, enjoying the sensation of me licking, sucking, and squeezing her. "Oh god, Nico. I didn't realize you got a magic tongue too."

I laughed, raking that very tongue over her nipples again. I liked it as much as she did. I wanted more though.

The windows were starting to fog in response to our heavy breathing. She threw her hand up, palming the glass as I released her breast with a wet pop. "I could suck your tits all night long and be happy about it, but I want that tight pussy again. Right now." Pulling her dress over her hips first, I leaned back, nodding for her to hop on.

She didn't hesitate, raising her hips and sliding onto my cock to the sounds of our collective groan. "Oh, that feels terrible," I said against her neck.

"Fuck," she breathed. "Lie to me more." She rocked forward and I grasped her hips to help her move. It felt so good, so right.

"Adam Foxx is the best human being in the world."

"Ah, more."

"The sky is red. My favorite food is broccoli."

"Yes. You have no idea how good it feels when you grow inside me."

I rocked my hips, meeting her thrusts. "I think I do. Can you handle more?"

"Yeah." She braced her hands on my shoulders, throwing back her head and making the dirtiest sound.

I decided to stop with the mundane lies and give her filthy ones instead. "Your pussy is like razors, shredding my hard wooden dick to sawdust."

She gasped, then laughed, then groaned, ramping up her pace as she rode me. I continued. "I'm so hard for you, I want to fuck you until that pussy is used up and spent." Okay, not a lie. Needed to be embellished. "Until it falls out and I can't fuck you anymore."

The windows were completely fogged now, and our bodies slapping together was our soundtrack. I was all over her, kissing her mouth, palming her breasts, thrusting myself inside her so deep I was hitting that spot. She bucked her approval and took every dirty kiss and moan like it was meant for her.

It was.

"You want me to give you more?" I breathed against her skin.

"No. I don't think I can handle another lie. You're filling me so good right now. I want to enjoy this before I come."

"I think you can take it bigger." Truth.

"I don't know."

I reached between us to finger her clit. She practically jumped out of her skin, reacting exactly like I wanted. I was so hard, so ready to come, but I wasn't done with her. Not yet. "I hate the feel of that tight pussy."

"Fuck me, yes. Nico, shit. Ah." The rest of what came out of her was unintelligible or maybe I wasn't hearing because we were so close to the edge and I'd grown so much it was like beautiful torture every time I pulled out and thrust back into her.

Just when we were about to finish, a knock on the window broke us apart.

Laurel jumped and I cursed. "Fuck. Be still. They'll go away."

"I know you're in there, Wood. And I know what you're doing. Roll down the window immediately."

Bubba Bettencourt.

Shit.

Laurel started fumbling with her halter, trying to get it tied when the door swung open. Guess we didn't think to lock it. I had other things on my mind at the time. She screeched and out of a desire to protect her, my hands flew to her tits, covering much more than her smaller hands would've.

Bubba leaned down, ignoring the obvious. "I told you both to stay on the straight and narrow, to follow the stipulations of your contracts. You failed. You're both fired and don't even begin to think you'll get any kind of severance or contract buy-out. You broke my rules. It's all forfeit."

I sucked in a breath to try to calm my rising heart rate. My career was over. So was Laurel's. I had to do something. "I know you don't approve of premarital sex, we are not engaging in a public setting. This is consensual private sex and who either of choose to have sex with is none of your business, Bubba."

"None of my business? Shucks. Everyone walking by here can see the car with the Tower bumper sticker on it rocking. You're fired. You won't change my mind about it. I don't care how good you are on the ice. I won't stand for these shenanigans with my club. Sex in the car, my good mercy me!"

He turned to walk away as the air left my lungs. I exchanged a harrowed look with Laurel, but she simply leaned out of the open door, calling out for him. "You can fire me, but I wouldn't fire Nico if I were you."

To his credit, he stopped, turning on his heel, but not approaching us like our sex would be catching. "I can do what I want with my team."

"Yes, that's true, but think for a minute what kind of press you'll get if you fire the disabled member of your team. He's making history with his penis replacement."

"He's not disabled. You've turned it around so nobody thinks it was true. He's been saying so for a week."

"Perhaps, but if he were to stop lying, to tell the truth about how lax security was on the night he was injured, which led to the tragic accident that could've claimed his life, it wouldn't be the best look. And if you were to fire the disabled member of your team, the press would be all over you, as well as multiple agencies who work for disabled rights. Not to mention, how the fans will react to losing their best player because he was having sex? You'll be ruined."

I sat there gaping at her and her brilliance. She had his balls to the wall and she did it all with my hands on her tits and my cock inside her.

#MagicalDicksDontLie

Chapter 12
Laurel

We were going all in. Not us, specifically, like as a couple, but us from a professional standpoint.

Bubba Bettencourt had called my bluff and fired me, but within seconds, Nico had re-hired me as his personal social media coach. Great for the bank account, but it sucked for my love life.

With me being his client, there was *no* way I could sleep with him again. It was a shame because the sex was amazing, not just the magic member, but he was something else. Sweet and dirty at the same time, and the way he used everything in his arsenal—hands, lips, tongue, hips—made for the best sex in my life.

Like, I said, shame.

But I couldn't do it again with him being my actual client. It was for the best to keep my professional walls intact.

I couldn't focus on that though. I had work to do because while Bubba followed through on my axing, he *did* believe my threat about Nico. He was still on the team and I'd called a massive press conference at the Tower to tell all of San Antonio and the world.

Nico looked killer in his black suit, white shirt, and Tower blue tie. The man was made for clothing and the way that everything he wore hung on him was what clothes designer dreams were made of. He could've been a model if he wanted. I could rattle off at least a handful of designers who would die to have him model their stuff. I'd make the formal list after the conference.

I had to get through that first.

He stepped up to the mic, looking equal parts confident and disarming. He was so good at that and it played well in the media. "Hey everyone. In case you don't know me, I'm Nico Wood, center for your San Antonio Tower and I'm here to do a bit of a confession. Are you ready to hear some tea?"

Definitely a natural.

The crowd of fans went nuts and the reporters in attendance went on high alert, ready for anything.

It's just what we wanted.

I scanned the crowd, making sure the Amputation Association and the American Foundation for People with Disabilities were in attendance. They'd brought some of their clients with them and as Bubba Bettencourt also checked out the support that had arrived for Nico, he looked like he'd rather screw a goat than be at this press conference.

Hashtag, too bad.

The laughs died down and Nico began his statement. I'd written something for him, but I knew as soon as I handed it to him, he wasn't going to read it.

"I'm here today to right a wrong. Against my better judgment, I lied to you. I could blame the team or Mr. Bettencourt, or even my social media guru, but it isn't their fault." He winked at me and as much as I tried to block the effects like a goalie stopping a slapshot, it wormed its way into my heart and I sighed. Just a little.

"As a responsible adult whose Mama taught me right from wrong, I chose to take the easy road and lie about my injury. Consequently, I've duped you all and I feel horrible about it. I'm here to make it right."

The crowd was mostly silent, save for a smattering of claps from the super fans. I expected that at first.

"Before I tell my story I need to make some things clear. Since there are kids here, there are certain words I should not say. I've been given a whole list of them, actually. For this discussion, imagine that male parts consist of two pucks and a hockey stick. Are you following me?" Most of the people laughed, some cheered and yelled. "Well, six months ago, I had my hockey stick severed by a skate."

He waited for the murmuring to die down before he continued. "Luckily, this didn't mean a life sentence of abstinence for me. I was taken to a doctor who specializes in stick reattachment. I was able to walk out of his clinic with a brand new hockey stick made of wood."

The murmuring crowd pressed forward, eager to hear more of the outrageous tale. They'd heard it before, but this time they were *listening.* He rested his elbow on the podium, looking perfectly comfortable with the delicate information. "I know, I said this before and retracted it. I'm sorry to say the retraction should never have happened. I owe this magic doctor everything for making sure I'd have a fulfilling life if you know what I mean, and lying about it was doing his work a disservice as well as doing a disservice to all of you out there who care about me and this team.

"There have been some adjustments getting comfortable with my new stick, but I want everyone to know none of this affects my gameplay. I am still a functioning capable hockey center who can handle not only *a* stick but both sticks." This time he winked at the crowd and they roared for him. Roared.

"I want to extend my sincere apologies for lying about this. I was fearful it would mean the end of my career, but Mr. Bettencourt and Coach Anthony have been nothing but supportive of me since the beginning of this ordeal."

Lie. That would feel good later.

Not to me, sadly, but some woman would benefit from that one. Maybe that blonde puck bunny from the restaurant.

"I'm going to open the floor for questions now. Remember to keep them PG-13."

All the hands in the room shot up. Nico wisely chose Hunter Cato first. This would be the test of how it was going to go. Everyone knew their history and if he handled whatever shit Hunter threw at him, he'd be golden.

Hunter cleared his throat, then held out his phone in that obnoxious way that said he was recording. "It's not physically or medically possible to reattach a di—hockey stick. You mentioned magic before. Are you saying there is actual magic involved in this procedure? You sound like an idiot."

Nico flexed his fists like he was going to vault over the podium and punch him. As he walked around the podium, I held my breath, hoping he wouldn't engage, but ready for it if he did.

When he reached the front of the stage we'd set up, instead of directly addressing Hunter, he turned his head to look right into my eyes. "I can't speak the specifics because I was obviously out during the procedure, but it sure feels like magic when I'm with the right person. That's good enough for me."

I swallowed, then turned all the way around so his piercing aqua eyes wouldn't see right through me. I'd told him we were keeping it professional. Several times. He didn't seem to get it.

Another reporter spoke up. A woman. "Can we get a peek?"

Nico chuckled. "You're going to have to use your imagination, I'm afraid."

I didn't doubt that many people would be doing exactly that. I did it way before I even saw it. Or felt it inside me.

I had to stop thinking like that.

Pro. Fessh. Ion. Al.

Nico took dozens more questions and handled them all beautifully. The press conference had been a success. The only one not happy about it was Bubba Bettencourt. He looked like he was going to throw up or throw Nico off the stage. He was quick to get out of there before anyone lobbed questions at him.

I busied myself with packing up the press packs we'd given out, getting the bulk of them stuffed in my bag before Nico sauntered over. "That went well, I think."

"Yeah, you did a good job. Keep up that story and Bubba will stay off your back for a while, at least until you make the playoffs next week." I hoisted my bag over my shoulder and started my trek to the car. "I'll see you soon, I guess. I'll text you if I line up any events for you. Have a great night."

Nico took my arm and swung me around. "No, no, Shadow. No running away from me."

"I'm not running. The event is over. Time to go plan the next one."

"So, I'll come with you, help you plan some things, then I can lie to you all night long."

I put my hands on his sculpted chest, shoving him back. "I told you."

"Yeah, yeah. You told me you want to keep things professional and between the lines and all the other ways you lined up, but my magical dick is telling me they're all lies."

Lie: Lying to Women Gets You Nowhere

Chapter 13
Nico

Laurel got a phone call from one of her team at the worst time. She was effectively able to scurry away from me due to some social media emergency that only she could handle.

It was utter bullshit. I was her only client and all my things were handled nicely.

She was avoiding me.

I get why she wanted to keep it professional, but there was no way I could do that, not with the chemistry we'd experienced. Not when I knew she was hiding behind that professional wall she'd built for herself.

If I wanted there to be more between us—and I did—then I would have to make her see reason and get over her reservations.

I was going to have to lie to her.

After I killed it at practice, even with Foxx being a distracted oaf the whole time, I showered, put on the clean gray sweats that I knew she dug, and went shopping.

I got some more flowers, not of the bribe variety. I wanted to buy the whole shop out, but Cato's mom convinced me it would be a little overwhelming. Plus, she needed inventory for other customers, so I stuck with some more fringe tulips, red this time.

Throwing them on the passenger seat of my SUV, I got out my phone to text Laurel.

Hey, sorry I was a dick today about your boundaries. I understand why we need to keep it professional now that I'm your client. I'll let it go since it's what you want. Friends?

My cock buzzed as it grew. Now that I knew what to expect, I noticed it happen. And I liked it.

Of course, everything I'd said in the text was a lie. I wasn't a dick, I didn't understand and there was zero chance of me letting it go.

It took her a few minutes to reply. The three dots were working overtime. I imagined her biting her lip as she thought of the perfect professional response and weighed that against how she really felt.

Shadow: Thanks for understanding. Of course, we're friends. I'm still coming to all your games and doing your press.

Nico: That makes me happy. Wait, not Mr. Happy. Just plain happy. Trying to follow your lead, like a professional puppet.

Shadow: Do you want to come over later to discuss the post-game scenarios? We need to prep something for a W or an L. (Not going to lose, just in case!)

This was the hard part. I wanted to answer yes, but I couldn't. Not if I wanted this to play out in the right way to show her she needed to let go and put a few cracks in her walls.

Nico: Can you handle that without me? I've got something going on tonight.

Lie. And maybe a bit of a play to make her jealous. It took her nearly ten minutes to reply to that one.

Shadow: Team stuff?

Nico: Nah.

That one probably got to her. I hope so anyway.

Shadow: That's fine. I'll handle it. See you tomorrow.

I took her reply as a win. She had no idea what was happening.

With her on the hook, I went about the rest of my shopping, sending her random texts—just like friends do—during the day.

Nico: I just saw a donkey walking down the sidewalk that looked like Foxx. I scared it off by throwing a stick at it.

Nico: I don't care what anyone says, peach cobbler is superior to apple. I said what I said. #lunch

Nico: Did you know my dad was a star center for the Cowboys back in the day?

Nico: I have a headache. I think I'm going to go take a nap. The last time I napped I was three years old!

Nico: Okay, the nap worked. My headache is gone. Yes!!!

Nico: I just realized I haven't vacuumed in three weeks.

Nico: I have 147 pairs of shoes. Too much?

Nico: Have you seen the blanket that used to be on my couch? It's missing.

Nico: I'm working on my biceps this afternoon. Be prepared for the gun show next time I see you.

Nico: I'm craving baked ziti for dinner.

Nico: My battery is almost dead. Forgot to charge. Email me if you need me.

She responded to every single text, but her replies got shorter and shorter each time. The last one about the battery got a thumbs-up emoji and that's it.

There was a slight chance I was pissing her off with this, but there was a bigger chance she was going to realize friend-zoning me was a bad idea.

I was a risk-taker, obviously—given the drunken naked hockey game that cut off my peen—and I was counting on the fact that I read her right and that our chemistry was going to win in the end.

After I'd gone about an hour incommunicado, I grabbed the dinner I'd made and packed up, scrawled a note on the card of flowers, and drove over to Laurel's condo.

Laying the flowers and card on the doorstep, I rang her bell and stepped to the side so she wouldn't see me when she opened the door.

I heard her open the card that read, *'I lied to you. All day long.'*

"Nico?"

I stepped out from the bushes, holding my cooler of food and wine. She was wearing a white cropped Tower tee and tiny blue shorts. Those things were hugging her hips in the best way. And that small sliver of stomach showing boiled my blood. The movement in my pants had nothing to do with lies then. I just craved her.

I waved my cooler. "The part about baked ziti was the truth. I brought some for you. The rest were lies though."

She took a moment to run her gaze up and down my body. It was only fair. I'd done it to her. When she got to the protrusion in my pants, she gasped but tried to smooth it over by going pure professional in her tone. "Traditionally when a man wants to be invited into my home, they call first and they don't start by admitting they've lied to me."

"It's time to make a new tradition."

"Nico, we can't—"

I interrupted her. "You're fired. Your severance pay will be the exact amount I was paying you weekly, for the next year. You can renegotiate after that."

She sighed. "You can't do that."

"I can and I did. We have no professional strings. I'm no longer your social media puppet." I dared to take a step toward her, closing in on the distance between us. "Don't act like you haven't noticed what I've got going on down here." I pointed at my wood. "Tell me to leave and I won't bring it up again."

Stopping her before the words she had locked and loaded on her tongue came out. "I don't think you're going to do that, though. I think you're going to realize our chemistry is too perfect to ignore and what we have is more than just a physical attraction to one another."

It took a few seconds of what I knew was a war in her brain, but she stepped aside, allowing me in. I pressed a kiss to her temple, as I set the cooler down. "Fuck first, eat later. Mr. Happy is ready to see you."

#WhenYouWantAJobDoneUseTheRightTool

Chapter 14
Laurel

Mr. Happy was not going to stick. I told him as much. He didn't seem to care. "Bedroom?" I pointed and he took my hand, pulling me inside, closing the door, and flicking on the light. "Undress."

I'd barely had time to fully think through my decision to let him in the house and he was already asking for the bedroom. I was not a zero-to-sixty kind of gal. "What?"

"You heard me. I've seen your body against the flickering film room lights and under street lamps. Right now, I want to see all of those beautiful curves in full living color."

He crawled on the bed and leaned against the headboard, tucking his hands behind his head, primed to enjoy the view.

I liked my body, curves, and imperfections included. I'd had boyfriends before, but none of them wanted to focus on me undressing. I was hesitant, at first, but the way he looked at me with those dreamy aqua eyes put me more at ease.

He'd been right. There was more to our chemistry than just the physical. I felt safe with him. And as I looked down at his dick, I felt thirsty for him too.

He'd lied a lot.

So much that I doubted I could handle it.

However, as he stared at me with his mouth practically watering, I realized I wanted to try.

I just had to let my walls down and do it.

Which was easier said than done. More than any man before him, I wanted to take our relationship further, but I'd been hiding behind a wall of my own creation for years.

He was about to knock it down with a wooden hammer.

I hooked my thumbs into the waistband of my shorts. Not what I would've been wearing if I'd known he was coming over, but the hunger, the raw desire in his gaze told me I was dumb to wait any longer.

I shimmied to loosen their grip and pushed them down to the ground, exposing my little purple panties. At least I had the good stuff on underneath.

He hissed his pleasure. "So pretty and sexy. Now the top, if you please."

Slowly, I raised the top over my head. I was starting to get turned on by the whole idea of this, especially when I noticed his cock getting harder.

Putting my back to him, I slid the tee over my head, throwing it toward him, and then turning around just as they hit his face. "You didn't even try to catch them." I scolded.

"Yeah, I was focused on your beautiful tits. Come here and let me show you how much I like them."

He slid down the bed, lying on his back, before pulling his sweats down to expose himself. The zing that ran straight to my core was so potent I flushed with heat. I couldn't wait to get my hands on him, so I slinked over and started to climb on. However, before I could get a leg up, my excitable cat shot out from under the bed. She was very protective of me and not used to strangers, so she attacked, leaping onto the bed with her claws out, taking one look at Nico's cock, and pouncing on it.

He howled as she sunk claws in his wood. I tried to shoo her away from him. "Cricket, no!"

My plea did no good. She was a cat, she had her claws out and eyes on the nice big piece of wood in front of her.

I reached out to push her off, but as I did, she dug her claws in deeper, making him shout. "Ah! What the hell?"

My heart thumped against my chest. My cat was about to claw my man's peen like a scratching post.

My man? Where did that idea come from?

Mentally, I felt the bricks of the wall I'd made crumble ". I'm so sorry. Let me just get her." I tried to pick her up, but she was still attached. Nico stared at me with wide eyes pleading for me to detach my cat, so I stroked the back of her neck, something that usually relaxed her. She calmed immediately and removed her claws.

Nico let out a puff of air, looking down to check himself. Cricket's response was to curl onto his stomach and begin licking her paw like she didn't almost send him back to Dr. Frankenpeen for a new cock. I bent down, looking for damage. "Are you bleeding?"

"Don't think so. She only got one claw in at the base. It's not as sensitive as the tip, but it sure as shit hurt more than when the dick doc whacked it with a hammer. What kind of monster is that?"

"Rescue cat. She likes to hop around instead of walking or running. It's why I named her Cricket."

"I'm going to call her Ginger Satan from now on." He reached down and stroked her neck like I had. "I hate cats." As he pronounced that massive declaration, his cock grew.

"Your dick says otherwise."

"Whatever. I think you owe me now. Your cat nearly mangled my junk."

"And what do you think I owe you? I can't help it if your manhood resembles a scratching post."

He cocked an eyebrow. "I'm sure you'll think of something."

I could think of a lot of somethings. All of them involved the nearly-mangled junk. "Are you sure you can—"

"Yes. I'm good. Move your cat before I do."

Lifting Cricket off of him, I went over to the door and set her in the hall. As soon as I closed the door again, a wall of heat brushed against my back and Nico's arms slid around my waist. I gasped in surprise. "I couldn't wait for you to get back to bed."

His want was so palpable. It was enough to crack nearly every remaining brick in my wall.

Was I really going to do this and give in?

He brushed my hair to the side and began kissing me, moving slowly across my shoulder and up my neck, flicking his tongue to taste my skin. I sighed at the sensation of it, at the burning tension it created in my stomach and core. "Lean back against me," he mumbled between kisses.

The moment I rested against his chest he slid his hand inside my panties, stroking me gently for a second—just enough to make me hot—then pushing his finger inside me. I bucked and he drew his finger back out, running it over my clit and back inside me again and again, as slow as possible. Or at least it felt that way.

Losing any small amount of control I may or may not have had, I moaned my agreement and moved my hips to meet the crawl of his fingers as he caressed me.

In the film room, we'd been rushed, screwing to get him through his size problem; in the car, we'd been desperate to see if there was something there. This was different. It was sensual, intense, sexy. I was surrounded by the heat of him, the scent of him, the feel of his tongue and fingers, and the deep growl of his voice as he shifted his hips and pressed his hardness against my ass. "Do you feel how hard I am for you?"

"You're cock's made of wood. You're hard all the time," I panted, pressing back against him and loving the way his length, his girth felt as he rode up and down my crack, sending little tremors of bliss through my body.

"No, Shadow. I'm not literally hard all the time, just when you're around. When we're close, you better believe my cock aches for you." His words had an even bigger effect on me than his grinding. The depth of his desire for me ignited a flame that I had no urge to put out.

As another mental brick in my wall shattered, I spun around, placing my hands on his shoulders. "Let me do something about that then." I pushed him toward the bed. He helped with his shirt and then there he was in all of his naked glory.

His body was the work of a god or the devil, I couldn't decide which. "Nobody should look this good naked."

He laughed, reaching out to stroke my cheek. "I'm glad you like what you see." Oh, I did. And then some. He dipped his head toward his sweats on the floor. "Wax. It's edible."

I grabbed the tin and opened it. The rich scent of cinnamon and ginger wafted into my nose. "Man, that smells delicious. No wonder I have the urge to lick you all the time."

Wrapping his hand around the nape of my neck, he pulled me down to him, kissing me with an honest need that made my head spin. That was who he was: honest and forthcoming, holding nothing back from me.

I'd forgotten where the wall had been. He pulled back we were both gasping, heaving with need. "No one is stopping you," he drawled. "And for the record, you have my standing permission to lick whatever you want whenever you want it."

I mean, what a nice gesture.

Dropping to my knees, I dredged a dollop of wax onto my fingers. He leaned back on his hands, watching with ravenous eyes as I slathered the wax on, running my hand over his large cock. He sucked in a breath as I hit that sensitive spot on the back where the tip met the shaft.

I was consumed with the idea of how great he was going to feel inside me, but first, I had to pay him back for Cricket's naughty behavior.

Leaning forward, I flicked my tongue over the tip, making circles and feathering over it with a light touch, with the taste of the wax bursting on my tastebuds. He moaned. "Damn, Shadow. You're not playing, are you?"

I was. I was playing with his dick like I was a cat and he was my toy.

Running my tongue up and down the length of him, first, I opened my mouth as wide as I could and sucked on the tip. His hips bucked. "As good as that feels, it's pretty big from all the lying, so don't feel like you need to—"

I cut him off by taking his cock into my mouth, deep-throating as best as I could. He was right, it was too big to get all the way in, but when the tip scraped the back of my throat we both hummed with pleasure.

His hands went into my hair, grasping and pulling as I bobbed up and down on his dick to the tune of his fuck yesses. When I began to suck as hard as I could with that mammoth in my mouth, he gripped harder. "That's the stuff dreams are made of. Your mouth is so hot and so eager. I'm blissing out here."

Taking the base of his dick in one hand and using the other to fondle his balls, I kept my mouth on the tip. The juxtaposition of flesh and wood was a pleasant sensation I hadn't even considered before then. He hummed his pleasure, then put his hand under my chin to ease the discomfort for me. "I'm okay. You don't have to assist."

"Are you kidding? I know your jaw must be hurting. Let me help you." I went back down on his cock, licking my way up and down while watching his aqua eyes heat. When I'd gotten my fill of that, I lowered my head to take him in again, choking and gagging a bit as he raised his hips. "Sorry. Your hot mouth just feels so good."

I shook my head, telling him not to apologize and the sound he made at that had me sticking my hand inside my panties. It was guttural, primal, and I took my cue and began to rock my head back and forth as he threw his back, enjoying the sensation. I was shocked when he pulled himself out. I raised an eyebrow, still trying to get back down on him. "Nope. That's not how this is going to end. Come here."

I stood, wiping my mouth which he seemed to like if his expression could be trusted. "As much as I want to come inside your mouth right now, we're going to do this together."

He laid me on the bed, kissing me, then trailing down to my breasts, sucking on each nipple until it was hard under his tongue. He murmured under his breath as he kissed down my stomach and pulled my panties off. "Your body is perfect. Your skin is so creamy and soft. I could spend a lifetime touching and kissing you without even getting my wood involved and die a happy man."

I raised, watching as his eyes skated over me, feeling the glide of his hands in the act of near-worship he was performing. "I like how you touch me."

He grinned, dipping down between my legs and licking my pussy. "You like this too."

"Mm-hm. I do."

He seemed to abandon all control, diving into me licking my clit, fucking me with his tongue, devouring me like it was a deep-seated need he had to satisfy. My hips bucked against his face and he pulled my legs apart, setting them on his shoulders so he could reach everywhere he wanted. He was ravenous. Dirty. Unrestrained and unstoppable.

Not that I wanted to stop him.

Just when I was close to that delicious wave of relief, he raised his head. I don't know what kind of face I made, but it made him chuckle. "All in good time, Shadow. I said we do this together."

He crawled up, positioning himself over me and placing that big, hardwood at my entrance. "Have I told you how ugly you are?" I opened my mouth to scold him, but his smirk stopped me.

Of course.

My hips raised as his cock grew more after the lie. "You ready for this?" He took his cock in his hand and rubbed it over my heated pussy. Yeah, I was ready for it. I just hoped I could handle it.

I bit my lip. "Mm-hm."

Grinning, he pushed inside, stretching me as his cock slipped in. The sting made spots appear before my eyes. "Good?" he questioned.

"Yep. So good. Move that big leviathan now, Nico. Please."

I didn't have to repeat myself. He placed his hands on each side of me and began—slowly—to thrust. I gripped his shoulders, my nails digging into his skin. I was going to apologize, but his groan told me he liked it.

It didn't take too long for me to adjust to his size. It wasn't abnormally large like in some romance books I'd read, but oh my devil-and-the-horse-he-rode-in-on, it filled me to my very limit. Every time he went deep, the sound escaping my throat was feral.

I didn't care. At all. Whispering to him because I couldn't catch my breath, "You can go harder."

He smirked, his eyes lighting. "Was that a suggestion or a plea?" He pushed, going so far inside it felt like it hit my eyeballs. I shuddered as chills erupted over my body. "Ah, plea then."

From then, he took control, hooking one leg over his hip so he could twist sideways—much like I'd done with his cock in my mouth—and drive in so hard, we both bounced off the bed a little.

"You feel so fucking right, Shadow. That tight pussy is just what I wanted."

I couldn't even respond he was pounding me so hard and I was so into it.

And it wasn't just the size of him—though that was a bonus—it was the way he looked at me, the way he touched me and sought permission or made sure my pleasure was as much as his. This guy cared about doing this right, not just about getting off.

He kissed me again, never stopping his hips in the process. As our lips and tongues and teeth fought for dominance our pace ramped up. I had to pull away from his kisses just so I could breathe. "You close?"

I bit my lip. "Good god yes, don't stop."

"I wouldn't dream of it." My hands flitted over his muscular back, his ass, his chest, anywhere I could find to touch. He pumped into me until I was panting. "You suck in bed," he murmured against my neck.

"What?"

"You suck in bed," he stated matter-of-factly. My fists curled as his cock grew inside me, filling me more. All I could do was hang on to him and let that sting travel all over my body and enjoy the tingles. "More," I breathed.

He reached down between us, flicking his fingers over my clit lightly and his wooden shaft railed me hard. "Your tits are...meh."

"I'd rather fuck Fuxx."

"I...I...I voted for Trump!"

He exploded inside me and I came right along with him. We gripped each other, kissing and humming our pleasure and riding each other until we came down from the high.

It was the best sex I'd ever had. In my life.

I couldn't believe I'd tried to hold him off in favor of professionalism. Jobs were not everything.

He was everything.

Lie: Whales Are The Biggest Animal

Chapter 15
Nico

I stood in the locker room door, hands on my hips and cock shoved nicely into my jock. The night before I'd "cleared out all the lies" with Laurel so there were no problems there.

She'd come around to the idea of us being together. No pun intended, and Mr. Happy and I could not be happier.

The only issue in my life was the playoff game. We had home advantage for the first round and I intended to make quick work of the Avalanche, but my mood was off because I'd taken a stroll around the stadium, one of the things I liked to do before playoffs. As I rounded the corner to the main entrance of the stadium where all the fans would be streaming through shortly, I discovered a massive display of Whalies Cereal free for the taking with the ginormous cartoon whale directly in front of the painting of my face.

The whole team was painted at the entrance and it was a big social media thing to stand by your favorite player and post a selfie with the hashtag, TowerPower on game day. There was no way any fan was getting close to my portrait thanks to that damned ginormous whale.

I balled up my fist to punch it in the beady eyes but was thrown off by a voice behind me. "I may have to keep you on the team, but I don't have to keep you in the game, Wood. You're out. Anttila is in."

I spun around to face Bettencourt, my fists still clenched. "You can't do that. This is the playoffs. I'm the captain and leading scorer."

"Not tonight. Your ass is on the bench, thanks to your antics. Just tell the world your private parts splintered or some such nonsense."

"Coach will never go for that."

"He will if he wants to keep his job." He tipped his cowboy hat and strolled off down the corridor, shouting over his shoulder, "You should have never tested me. Have fun watching the game." That left me to bloody my knuckles on a fiberglass whale.

After I mangled the whale, I sprinted back to the locker room, eager to discuss things with Coach Anthony, who told me exactly what Bettencourt had. If he didn't bench me, he was out of a job.

I felt for the guy and begged him to go against Bettencourt, but he responded by getting out his phone and showing me pictures of his six kids.

Damn, Bettencourt. We never figured he would go this far with it. My only hope was the fans rebelling during the game.

Coach Anthony blew his whistle, starting his new playoff pregame ritual. Each team member was to read a book of their choice before the game. I'd picked a sports memoir from San Antonio's first star center, some of the other guys had other sports-related books, and some had fiction.

I don't think any of us were actually reading our books though. Our heads were on the game. Well, theirs were. Mine was going over how to get my ass back on the starting lineup.

Sighing when I came up with nothing, I looked up and spotted Fuxx. He had a book, but it didn't look like a regular book. He was writing in it, scribbling things down, poking around on his phone, then scribbling more things.

He probably wanted it to look like he was journaling or taking notes, but I would bet my brand-new wooden cock he was working out bets. It wasn't my business, but as captain and leader of the team, it was my job to make sure everyone was focused and ready, even if I wasn't going to be on the ice.

If he was worried about his wagers all night, that could and would get sticky for us. "Hey, Foxx. Is your head in the right place?"

He ignored me, scribbling on the book. "Yo, Fuxx. I'm talking to you." He looked up, an angry scowl on his face. "I said is your head in the game?"

"Yes, it is motherfucker. You worry about yourself and your stick." He slammed the book shut and threw it in his locker before storming out of the locker room.

Two minutes before the second period was over, we were down, three to one, which is what happens when you don't let your best player on the ice. The team itself was performing fine, but as I'd suspected, Foxx was a shitshow, missing a couple of easy slapshots that he should've been able to stop in his sleep.

Every time he'd missed stopping a goal, he looked up to the stands to Hunter Cato. Hunter was on his phone the whole time, nodding or holding up one or two fingers.

I knew what that was about. It was obvious.

As the clock counted down from ten, one of the Avalanche got around O'Brien and eased a puck straight at Foxx. My six-year-old niece could've blocked the shot, but Foxx glanced up at Cato and twisted, letting the puck sail right past him without even trying to disguise it much.

Four, one.

I tore off the bench and blasted past the team to get to Foxx who was firing toward the locker room before the coach came in to yell himself hoarse at our gameplay.

"What the fuck are you doing?"

He shoulder-checked me, ignoring my question and hurrying for his locker. Where was *that* hustle during the game?

I wasn't going to stand around and take that, so I grabbed him by the jersey and pulled him up to face me eye-to-eye. "I asked you a question. What is going on with you and Cato?"

"Stand down, Wood." Coach Anthony. He pushed me away and glanced to my usual spot on the bench in front of my locker proceeding to stand there and spittle me to death with his angry "pep talk."

Knowing it had nothing to do with me, I focused on Fuxx who was also preoccupied with other things. That damn book he'd been writing in before the game.

I stood up, acting like I was stretching out my hamstring—like I needed to—and got as close as I could get to see what he was up to.

The entire two-page spread was covered in lines and numbers. It was a betting sheet, just as I thought. As I looked closer I saw our team, his and my names specifically, and a lot of calculations that I didn't get.

That fucker was placing odds on our game.

That was one of the biggest fucking no-no's in the rules. I reached for the book, intending to out him to the coach, but I must have given myself away because just as I snatched at the book, Fuxx shoved his skate right between my legs.

He didn't even make contact, but the trauma from the accident must have been lying dormant in my head because I shuffled, trying to get away and ending up falling on the floor like an ass.

At least this time my cock stayed connected.

Everyone had a good laugh at my expense, but I didn't care. Much anyway. I just wanted to get rid of Foxx. "Coach, you need to put Stoker in. Take Foxx out."

The coach sighed. "I don't know what you two have going on between you, but as captain, you need to be the bigger man here, Wood. I'm not subbing him out for a rookie who doesn't have a playoff under his belt. No offense, Stoker." Stoker looked relieved. "Leave Foxx alone."

"But he's—"

"I don't care. It's hard enough without you out there. If I take Foxx out, it'll be worse. Now, be the captain I know you are." Frustrated, I had no choice but to let it go.

Normally I would've been the guy to expose the truth and damn the consequences, but this time if the truth got around to the NHL, our season would be forfeited and my career even more scrutinized than when I came home with a wood knob. So I chose to keep it under wraps for the moment, round up the team, and put our hands in. It took me a second to clear my mind and find something productive to say, I was so irked over Foxx, but I dug deep, knowing they were counting on me. "I hate like shit that I'm not out there, but I'm out there, okay? I'm with you. You can do this. Don't let the motherfuckers have the puck. Tower on three. One, two, three, Tower!"

As the team filed out for the last period, I went over to Foxx's locker to grab the book. Coach caught me. "What are you doing by Foxx's locker Wood? I told you to get away from him. Now get out here!"

I grabbed my phone quickly. "I'm coming. Just a sec."

Since I wasn't going to play, I stuffed my phone under my gear so I could take it out and text Laurel discreetly when the action started again.

Nico: I need you to sneak into the locker room and get a brown book from Foxx's locker.

Shadow: Is there a reason why I'm committing a crime?

Nico: I think he bet against us with Cato and is throwing the game. I need proof. Couldn't get it myself.

Shadow: Oh shit. That's against the rules, isn't it? Of course, it is. I'll see what I can do. What should I do with the book when I get it?

Nico: Take it to Bettencourt. He'll yank his ass so we won't get fined or DQ'd. The damage is done, but if we can keep the NHL reps from catching on, maybe we'll be okay.

Shadow: Look at you leading the team without being in the game. I'll reward that behavior later. ;-)

Sounded like a winner of an idea, so I shot her a thumbs-up emoji, then stashed my phone and headed back out to watch the game like the loser I felt like I was.

Cat Collins

#AidingAndBetting

Chapter 16
Laurel

Sneaking into the locker room while the game was on proved to be easier than I thought it would be. I'd been a familiar face and none of the guys left in there seemed to be onto the fact I was technically fired, so I was able to stroll in saying I needed to leave something for Nico, grab the book, and get out without so much as a second glance.

As I made my way toward the private box where Bubba Bettencourt was watching the game, I thumbed through the book. It was full of bets Foxx had made in the past and those coming up in the future. The most used page based on the marks was in the middle. He was figuring and refiguring a huge amount of money. If he owed that much to Hunter or any other bookie, I didn't see how he could pay it. It was in the millions.

And I also didn't think Hunter Cato had the brains or funds to be the one to benefit from Foxx's losses. He was probably just the contact.

I got an idea and turned on my heel. Maybe I could figure out what was going on if I questioned Hunter before I exposed Foxx to Bubba.

Finding him in the press box, I called him over. "What do you want Laurel, to cry about your boyfriend being benched? If you ask me he got what he deserved."

"No, he didn't. He's being discriminated against, but I'm not here to talk about Nico. I want to talk about Adam Foxx."

He turned, looking over at Foxx as he stood guard in front of the net, eyes glued not on the action, but on us. Hunter glanced at his phone, then made a subtle peace sign and held it behind his back. Nico was right. There was definitely something happening here. "What about Adam? I need to focus on the game."

I took a chance, baiting Hunter with something I knew would get his attention. "Nico was thinking of giving you an exclusive on Sports

Blender, you know? Imagine if you're the one to break the story of why he's not playing today."

Bingo.

He swung back around, putting his call on mute and dropping his arm, causing his phone to dangle at his side where I could see the screen. "He despises me."

"That doesn't matter. I've told him the social media ramifications would be huge if he were to go on Sports Blender and make amends for punching you and give you the exclusive. He listens to me and he'll do it."

Nico was going to hate that, but I could smooth it over with him. We both knew something was going on here besides wagering money on his own game. We needed the scoop.

"What do you want to know about Adam?"

"He's up to his gonads in debt, right?" Hunter nodded as I peeped down to his phone. "I'm guessing loan sharks are after him?" Again, a nod. "Who is he indebted to? Who's his bookie? I need names." If we were going to keep the team off the NHL radar, we needed to know who was involved.

He shook his head. "I don't know and I wouldn't tell you if I did. The guy is dangerous and powerful." He was lying. I would've known even if I hadn't just figured out what, exactly, was going on.

"So, Adam is fixing the game in real time. You're relaying messages to him so that people who are betting can bet on small moves, not just the outcome of the game."

"I can't confirm or deny that."

I patted his chest. "You just did. Thanks."

Turning, he grabbed my arm to stop me. "We had a deal. Wood will do my show?"

"Yeah, sure. See ya."

I wasn't sure at all. I'd leave it up to Nico. It wasn't a half-bad idea I'd had, media and reputation-wise, but the reason he wasn't in the game was now a moot point.

Grabbing my phone, I shot him a text.

Shadow: Start warming up. You're going in.

Lie: Good Guys Never Win

Chapter 17
Nico

I had no idea what Laurel had done, but roughly one minute after her text, Coach Anthony called me and the third-string goalie, Stoker over. "Just got word. You two are going in."

Finally. Sitting there watching my team fumble was killing me. Even if we ended up losing after all, at least I'd know I'd done what I could to stop it.

Pulling Stoker up by the neck of his jersey, I got in his face. His eyes had gone wide with fear the second the coach had told him he was going in. "You've got this. Do you hear me? It's just one period." He nodded and we burst out onto the ice.

Fuxx skated right up to me, pulling off his gloves and going for my face. I deflected his blows and laughed. "You should be kissing me instead of punching me, Fuxx."

"What's that supposed to mean?"

"We just saved your ass from a fine and suspension. You're welcome."

I left him behind taking my place on the ice, where I was meant to be. The fans erupted. I'd never heard the noise level so loud before. Glancing up to the box, I spotted Laurel with her arms crossed, sitting next to Bettencourt who looked like he was about to puke. I slapped my stick on the ice, letting her know I was proud of whatever she'd done.

I'd reward her later.

The whistle blew and I was back in the game.

I slammed a goal in within the first minute. I was so pumped, so determined and I gave zero shits how many of the Avalanche I had to mow down to make it happen.

O'Brien skated over to me, jumping on my back and hugging me like I was his puppy dog. "So glad you're back in, Wood. Let's do this."

Four, two.

Two plays later, I shot him the puck and he landed the goal by clipping the defender, banking right, then slamming the puck in.

Four, three.

This was what great hockey looked like.

The Avalanche started to fall apart right in front of us. I don't know if it was the exuberant crowd, my presence, or the way the team had perked up when I came in. They were losing it.

So much so that three fights broke out before the ref could settle us back down and get the game going again.

All the while, Fuxx sat on the bench with his head in his hands, not daring to look up at the game or Hunter Cato.

Thirteen minutes in, Parker stole the puck and took it down the ice. I could pick his new wife out of the crowd by her screaming. He got in a jam, shot the puck to me, and then flew around the Avalanche player, so I whacked it back and he deked, deflecting it straight between the pipes.

Four, four.

It was insanity in that stadium.

I glanced up. Laurel was jumping up and down, tits bouncing, and Bettencourt was on his phone with his back turned.

For the next twelve minutes and fifty-four seconds, we battled back and forth. I almost had a couple of goals but was thwarted by the Avalanche goalie. One of their players took advantage of the momentary resettling of the teams and took off down the ice toward our goal with a clear breakaway.

Stoker was at his post. Staring down the player with something akin to terror in his eyes. I could almost see the calculations in his mind. If he doesn't block the incoming shot, they'll win. There's not enough time for us to score the tie.

My heart thumped in my chest as I sped toward him. I was the fastest NHL player on record, so I never doubted my ability to catch up to the breakaway.

I did, however, doubt Stoker's ability to have confidence in himself. He was shuffling back and forth, his eyes glazing over as the player toyed with him.

I had a choice. I could try to stop the player or I could try to stop the puck.

Making that decision at the last nano-second, I slid into the area right above the crease, spreading my legs wide and hoping for the best. He slapped the puck at the same moment, sending it right into my groin.

I fell over the puck as the buzzer sounded, staying there and holding my breath as the team crowded around me to celebrate.

My pecker was good. Didn't even feel the strike with my jock in place. It was more of a metaphorical statement than anything. I'm not sure I would've made the same move before my cock replacement surgery.

The crowd cheered and the Avalanche needed a moment to regroup. We still had overtime to go, but I wasn't worried about our chances.

Laurel rolled over, stretching out and looking like Ginger Satan did after her cat naps. We were in my massive king-sized bed and as the sheets fell off her breasts, my wood stood to attention. Nuzzling next to her, I kissed her neck. "It sucked to lose the Stanley Cup."

She giggled. "Did I fuck your brain out last night? You won it by a landslide."

"Mm, did we? I don't think so."

She sighed as I pressed my now-growing cock against her ass. "Oh yeah, remind me again what happened. Lots of details please."

Fondling her boob with one hand and roaming my hand over the perfect curve of her hips and ass, I purred in her ear. "We lost the first game, so we were out of the playoffs, Fuxx made his loan shark payments with money to burn, getting a medal from the NHL for his illegal activities and Bettencourt's whale crawled up my ass and died."

She hissed as my hand found her swollen clit. We'd done some celebrating through the playoffs and the final too, but it was never going to be enough to satisfy my need for this woman.

In reality, the Tower scored the overtime goal, taking us to the next playoff game, and the next, all the way to the matchup with the Rangers, Foxx was fired and was on the run from the loan sharks, and in the most shocking turn of events, Hunter Cato ended up accidentally responsible for Bubba Bettencourt's ass rotting in a jail cell.

He'd snuck into Bettencourt's private toilet to use the "good john" during a practice game and overheard a phone call in which Bubba was shouting over the phone about the production lines on Whalies being too slow in the Harbor House facility.

With Harbor House being the name of one of his orphanages, Hunter did some digging and discovered Bettencourt's use of child labor. He sent in an anonymous tip and Bubba was arrested. Turns out Mr. Clean was a very dirty guy. With him gone, the betting ring dissolved and the NHL never got wind of anything.

Was it a bit dishonest to keep the illegal betting in the playoff game under wraps?

Yeah, well, lying always worked out well for me, so...

Laurel moaned as I picked up her leg, hiking it back and hooking it over my hip, giving myself access to that sweet spot of hers. "The sky is red. Sharks make great pets. My parents are coming to stay and meet you next week."

"Wait, what?" She stilled, trying to tell if my cock grew or not, and when it did, she relaxed.

"Thank goodness," she sighed.

"Yeah, they're coming in two days, but don't worry about that. Worry about this."

I pushed inside her tempting depths. She was already hot and wet and the grunt we both made at my size filling her was music and playoffs and rain on a hot day.

"I don't worry about your cock," she sighed. "Lie to me."

I pulled her chin, forcing her to face me so I could sweep my tongue over her bottom lip. She loved that, and she loved when I began to kiss her in earnest, slanting my mouth, and breathing all my emotions into her. She always matched me, whether it was soft or like then, nearly bruising, opening her mouth, and inviting my deepest self in.

When I pulled away, I leaned my forehead against hers. "I detest the taste of you, and those sounds you make are awful. Really, I hate you, if I'm being honest."

She gripped my arm, as our bodies slapped together in rhythm. "I hate you too," she rasped, her nails digging into my arm as she hung on.

Reaching down, I gave her what she needed to finish, playing with her clit with one hand and grasping her hip with the other, our breaths getting faster and our hands and bodies desperate to come. "Fuck," she yelled, throwing her head back, making her hair cascade over my shoulder. I'd never felt closer to a woman—hell, a person—in my life.

It was like she was carved out of my dreams and put in front of me to love and care for. As her pussy clenched over my wood, I vowed to pull her strings as long as I could.

Epilogue. Truth: Lying Never Felt So Good

Five years later.
Start of Hockey Season.
Nico

I stood five feet out of frame in Hunter Cato's studio, delivering on a promise Laurel made five years ago. I'd put it off because I had trouble forgiving the guy who took part in something that could've tanked my team and career, but he'd come through for us more than enough to prove himself once he got away from Adam Fuxx's influence.

"Today on Sports Blender we've got an interview that's a long time coming. As promised, chatting with me will be the one and only San Antonio Tower captain and superstar, Nico Wood. Come on in and say hey, Wood."

"Hey, Hunter. Sorry, it took so long for me to get here. I was busy winning the Stanley Cup twice, endorsing products for the penally challenged, proposing to my girlfriend, getting married, and going to Paris for the honeymoon. You know, things." All true. Every word. It had been an amazing period in my life. All thanks to a horrific accident that started the ball rolling. As strange as it was, I was thankful that my penis had been severed.

"I see. Speaking of endorsing products, how do you respond to the notion that you single-handedly made erectile dysfunction cool?"

"First of all, there is nothing dysfunctional about my wood, let me get that clear. Ask my wife if you need confirmation. But when I took those ED endorsements, for me, it wasn't about the money. It was about those few minutes as I lay there looking at my dick five feet away and wondering how it got over there. The trauma it caused in just those few minutes was unbelievable. I wanted people to know how lucky they are, even if they're manhood suffers an unfortunate accident. There are ways to overcome it.

113

"Listen, we take ibuprofen when our muscles hurt, and Cough syrup for colds, why not take a pill when your cock is floppy? It's all just a part of your body. And if I had any role in bringing the conversation into the mainstream, then that makes me happier than winning another Stanley Cup would."

Not really. I mean, it's the fucking Stanley Cup.

His eyes widened. "Your endorsements certainly have helped you make enough money to do whatever you want with the rest of your life. Any word on your retirement and what happens after you hang up your skates?"

"I'm weighing my options, got my eye on a club to buy after I leave the NHL. It might be nice to see what the world's like on the other side of the ice, you know? And it's time for us to think about having kids. I want to be a present father and husband to my wife, so maybe if we win the cup this year..."

"You're saying you'll retire after the cup? That's big news and you're breaking it here. You heard that, right listeners?"

I knew that would get him pumped. As annoying as he was, I did owe him something for coming clean with Laurel when she discovered what Bubba Bettencourt and Fuxx were doing. "I'm thinking about it. I can't make decisions like this without Laurel's input and we haven't had that conversation fully yet."

"Fair enough. Let's talk about your unique penis, shall we?"

"It's all anyone ever wants to talk about, but hey, I don't mind. It's a part of me now and like I said, normalizing what happened is a good thing."

"You've already told us it still functions properly. Any changes to that? Is the wood holding up well? And for the love of all women everywhere, I've wanted to know this since day one: what about splinters?"

"That's my most asked question. No splinters. I have a special wax that coats my wood and makes the possibility of splinters nil. It's quite nice and smells great. In fact, I've entered into a partnership with Dr. Frankenpeen and Sweet Cosmetics to design a line of aftershave and skin products to sell to the general population who haven't been dismembered. We discovered early on that the wax doesn't just work well for its intended purpose. Laurel says it's better than any lotion she ever had on her hands, so we're going to sell it with the doctor's permission and input."

"You're going to produce and sell the same stuff you slather on your dick?"

I chuckled. "In a way. Our company will be called Bleu Fairy, and we'll carry men's and women's products in a variety of scents. All of our products will be safe, organic, and perfect for bedroom scenarios. I've brought some prototypes for you today." I mentally patted myself on the back for remembering the verbiage she'd given me, word for word.

"That's awesome. Thanks so much. I'm wondering why you won't give out his contact information or put it all over the internet for others. I've done extensive searches for this guy and came up empty-handed. He seems to be a ghost and off the grid completely. Surely others could benefit from his techniques, so why not share?."

"I'm afraid I can't do that, Hunter. I signed an NDA, and I was given knock-out meds to keep me from knowing the location of his clinic after I left anyway. Dr. Frankenpeen is an enigma. If you need him, he'll find you. That's all I can say. Now, if you will excuse me, I have to go clean out my gutters, build a boat, and pick out my Halloween costume. Thanks for having me today."

None of those things were true and I figured everyone listening knew it. Especially Laurel. It was my little message to her, telling her to get ready for me to lay some wood.

"Hold it. You know the deal, Nico. This is the Sports Blender. What did you bring with you for me to blend up?"

Damn. I was hoping he'd forget about this part. "Right. I almost forgot. Here you go. This stick signifies my wood, of course. Have at it." I pulled a stick from my pocket, handed it to Hunter, then stepped back as he chucked it into his blender and turned it on.

This was his thing, and he was still doing it five years later. Even though it was ridiculous as shit. Once a golf pro threw a golf ball in there and ended up giving himself a concussion.

Bits of wood flew out, making us both turn and wince, but when he'd gotten it blended to finely ground sawdust, he poured it out on the table. "That's the blend of the day. See you next time."

After I tossed him a bag of our new products, I beelined home to Laurel. She greeted me at the door wearing one of my jerseys. It hung down to her knees and I knew she had nothing on underneath. Mr. Happy was super pleased about that.

I stepped through the door, but instead of jumping into my arms and kissing me like I expected, she slugged my bicep, punctuating every word. "How. Did. You. know?"

"Know what?"

"You mentioned kids. Why?"

"Oh, that? I was just trying to think of lies. Gutters, boats, kids, you know." I grabbed her waist and nuzzled against her neck, breathing her in and appreciating what a lucky bastard I was. "Wait. Wy are you asking about kids?"

She slapped my ass and ran toward the bedroom. I had to practically kick Ginger Satan out of my way to follow her. I bolted down the hall and burst into the room. "Are you pregnant?" She shrugged. "You are. You're pregnant."

I bounced over, throwing her over my shoulder and slapping her ass before tossing her onto the bed. She giggled as I threw myself over her. "You better not be lying to me."

A sexy smirk spread across her lips. "And you better be lying to me."

More Dr. Frankenpeen novellas to come soon, but while you wait, be sure to check out my Urban Fantasy, READ BETWEEN THE GRINDS. It's short (230 pages), full of spice and humor, much like WOOD.

Two women. Two stories. Once curse.

Fallon's Light Roast: Having a wreck and getting a ticket were just the beginning of my problems. Wait, no, just the beginning of my curse, if you could believe that nonsense. I didn't have the time or the brainpower to believe in curses. I had a new coffee shop to run and bills to pay, including a ticket for the wreck I didn't cause. Imagine my surprise when I started seeing people's futures in their coffee cups. Didn't have a choice about believing in that stupid curse then. When I saw the future of my hottest customer featuring me on my, ahem, knees, I suddenly wasn't sure if disbelieving was a good thing. That was definitely a future I could support.

Esme's Black Tea: Everyone in Between knew about the witch's cursed bird. Heck, my family's business profited every time that bird appeared. I just never thought it would show up in my life. At the worst time ever. I'd been on my way to break up with my boyfriend and put Between in my rearview when the Wayward Warbler struck, chaining me to the town until I got rid of the curse. I figured it would be easy, but when I started actually seeing people's pasts in my tea leaves, including the grease monkey fixing my car and the past we'd shared, easy was the last thing   that   it   was.

Welcome to Between, Nevada, where the residents know there are two sides to every curse.

This is a steamy novel for mature readers that contains two overlapping stories—one with light rom-com vibes and the other one dark. Together they tell a complete tale. For CW, please check the author's website.

If you're looking for a series featuring the same couple, check out my DIMINISHING MAGIC series. It's complete with four books and has some of my same signature humor with lots of spicy heat. It's a paranormal romance featuring a gnome—yeah, I said gnome, and no she doesn't have a pointy red hat—and a wolfhole. Her quest the join the magical Conclave is blocked by the hot wolfhole with glowing purple eyes who's designed a series of trials for her to prove her worth. If she doesn't, he will have to kill her.

This story starts with a slow burn, but the spice heats up as the books progress. It's got a pack of hot wolves, a horny bi fairy, magical obstacles, and a feisty female main character with a quick wit and sharp tongue the wolfhole can't resist.

   And if you're in a very festive mood, you could always check out my Christmas Why Choose romance featuring Vixen, one of Santa's naughty reindeer shifters. The book has naughty & nice games, three different men who want to help Vixen get over her broken heart that Rudy, the reindeer has broken into pieces. It features ice play, spanking, a unique piercing, a magical tongue, candy cane crossing (MMFM), and a sleigh ride you won't forget. One reader says, "I'll never look at Jingle Bells or Rudolph in the same way again and that's a good thing!" The next book in this series comes out Christmas 2024

A Word on Reviews

Indie authors rely on readers. It's as simple as that. We cannot keep publishing if no one knows about our books. The big corporate river which shall not be named doesn't help authors but the biggest of the big. You know the ones. I don't even have to name them.

I can't stress enough how important leaving reviews on Amazon (Oops, I just named them) are. Books must have AT LEAST 50 reviews before Amazon pushes them "organically." (Meaning, without author paying hundreds of dollars on advertising.) This is where YOU, dear cherished reader can help.

If you enjoyed WOOD (or even if you didn't) please take a few minutes to post a review. (Note simply rating this with stars does not equate in the algorithms.)

IT MATTERS.

Don't know what to write in a review? Say what characters you liked, tell what tropes you found, compare it to other books, tell how it made you feel, talk about the spice or character development or talk about how silly you thought it was. Anything. Seriously.

I mean, don't put that you think I'm a dumbass for writing it, please. But other than that, just give your basic thoughts. Click a star level, then move on with your day knowing that this gal is probably checking Amazon more often than she should & when she sees that review you just wrote? YOU have made me happy & made a difference in her life & career.

SEE HOW MUCH POWER YOU HAVE??

No, go forth & change the world. Here's the QR code to review WOOD.

THANK YOU TIMES A ZILLION. LET ME KNOW IF I CAN BOOST A SOCIAL MEDIA PAGE TO PAY IT BACK!

ACKNOWLEDGEMENTS & A WORD FROM THE AUTHOR

So, this was a little different, no? I hope you enjoyed this humorous (unrealistic) take on the hockey romance genre. And, you know, all the penis talk. I had so much fun writing it and spent more time than I want to admit looking up synonyms for penis. The idea for this novella came from an innocent post in a Facebook group wherein the poster asked for a "Magic Puppet Whose Nose Grows" rec. My mind went straight to this.

You're welcome...?

Please accept my apologies for any hockey irregularities I may have written into this story. Sometimes you bend reality to fit fiction. No offense to all the hockey fans and players out there. I've just learned how hot and fun hockey is, but if I committed any grievous hockey sins, please forgive me.

Special love to my Street Team for spreading the word for me. I appreciate all your comments and posts!

Thanks to everyone who read an ARC draft of this work. And even more thanks if you posted a review afterward. I cannot do this without the support of my readers who review, so I appreciate you more than I can express.

I'd also like to thank all the readers who weren't afraid of a few peen references.

As always, thanks and appreciation to my friend, crit partner & owner of half of my brain, Mandy O'Dell. And to my family for being okay with me venturing into this territory. Just don't tell Mamaw about this one, please!

ABOUT THE AUTHOR

Cat Collins is the #1 bestselling author in her home. No really, her husband wrote a training manual for work once. Sold one copy to his boss. She writes what she likes to read: swoony alphas, witty dialogue, and steamy scenes that make your heart (and various other parts) flutter.

Her Diminishing Magic series has garnered praise from reviewers and a 5-start Readers' Favorite review for its hilarious banter, sexual tension between characters, and turns you never see coming. Described as a "twisty bundle of fun," and a "rollercoaster ride you won't want to get off," the series includes elemental magic, wolf shifters, and a main character who's full of sass.

A reading interventionist by day and, reader and binge-watcher by night, Cat lives in the Southern US with her aforementioned husband, two kids, and two cats, one of whom likes to edit as Cat is writing by jumping on the keyboard unexpectedly. Any stray typos must certainly be the work of Poe.

She loves connecting with readers on social media. Find her as @CatCollinsBooks on TikTok Facebook, & Instagram. Join her private reader group on Facebook at Facebook.com/groups/cattalesreaders

Made in the USA
Columbia, SC
29 July 2024

39628139R00068